The Keeper's Warrior

by
Christina "Smudge" Hanson

Cover and interior illustrations
by Christina "Smudge" Hanson
SmudgeMarks & EngelWerks
http://www.smudgemarks-engelwerks.com

Published by Fox Den
http://www.rindis.com/fox-den

Offering to Euseeda

For over a month, his entire world consisted of blue skies, screaming seabirds and the briny taste of the ocean spray that clung to the insides of his mouth. But soon, he'd have a reprieve. The ship he had traveled on had finally made dock in a tiny port-side town. It needed supplies for the rest of the journey so the stopover here would be brief. Just long enough to unload some minor cargo, take on fresh water and food, then take the next available tide back out in the morning. But it would be long enough to do a little exploring in town, maybe even get a drink of something other than the foul swill the sailors guzzled. He was not going to pass this by.

He stood on the edge of the ship's deck, waiting anxiously for the gangplank to drop. Solid ground was calling him. As he waited with long-sword and short-sword scabbard on his hip, knife tucked behind in the small of his back, he shifted his duffel bag across his shoulder, in an attempt to have it lay better across his back-slung shield, then looked out over the port.

It was more a fishing village than true trade port; a small deep cove harbor, with one all-wood pier to moor. The township itself was maybe a few buildings deep, and of those, mostly warehouses and a spattering of dock maintenance workshops. Behind them, stairs rose out of solid rock and stretched to the

1

upper levels of the town, which tiered itself along the cliff-side for at least three more levels. Half-timber houses and shops lined the cobblestone streets as they snaked higher up the receding cliff-face.

But what really caught his attention was to the southeast. An extra crag jutted out over the already high town, its slopes surrounded by dense green, with an open area on top of which a small building stood, its top covered by the canopy of a great tree. He knew exactly what that was.

A shrine to Euseeda.

The corner of his lip ticked up briefly in a soft smile, then disappeared as quickly as it came. It had been some time since he had been able to give an offering to his goddess of the earth. Now was as good a time as any.

The plank hit the pier hard and bounced before settling still. One boot in front of the other, and the tinny rattle of chain mail in his ears, he strode off the ship and into the township of Echo Cove.

The town was much bigger than he first thought, streets and buildings stretching beyond the edges of the cliff. While it was nowhere near as big as many of the cities that he had marched through, it was indeed prosperous in its isolation. The drinking water flowed clean from the fountains that were dotted around the place, and the streets were bare of the typical smell of sewage. Now that he was higher, he could see beyond the township to rolling farmland fields. They were packed with abundance and heavy stalks of grain danced in the gentle breeze. Everything here seemed green and alive, despite the oncoming of the fall harvest. He crossed very few people as he made his way, as most were out in the fields beyond, or taken to sea for the day's catch. But those he did, smiled and greeted him with pleasant "Good Day"s or

"Howdy"s.

"Euseeda has blessed this land greatly," he muttered to himself.

He finally reached the steps to the shrine and stopped. From where he stood, they looked dizzyingly steep. For a moment, he contemplated turning back. He still had his sea-legs and the world seemed a bit unsteady. But he had walked farther, climbed higher, and trudged through far worse things than this shrine's pathway. He couldn't properly call himself a sell-sword if something like this hindered him. Taking a deep breath, he began his ascent. Around him, trees danced on the edge of the path, their leaves softly chiming as they brushed against each other in the coastal breeze. The woods here were thick and lush. It was hard to see very far past the sides of the granite steps. Roots reached and tangled within the grooves of the stones, yet remained clear enough to insure a good perch for a climber's foot.

When he finally reached the top, he paused just under the small arbor that marked the sacred ground's true entrance, letting himself catch his breath. While the climb probably would not have been much effort for him regularly, his time being lazy on-board ship was telling. Being dressed in his full, heavy plate and chain did not help the matter. But he was not about to leave all his worldly possessions unguarded. Plate was easier worn than carried. After a moment, he straightened himself out, readjusted his bag on his shoulder, then continued into the courtyard of the shrine.

The courtyard itself was full of sunlight, open and airy. The ground around the shrine was rich with green grass that was trimmed just shy of stones set into the earth as a pathway. Chest-high bushes ringed the entire area, insuring that no visitor would accidentally fall off the top, short of the stairs that lead here. In the center was the shrine, little more than a square walkway of wooden pillars with leafy capitals and a simple peaked, red-clay tiled roof surrounding an open air atrium. Inside the atrium, a tree of Euseeda rose, dominating nearly all of the space, its large canopy rising past the roof to cover the entire building. Behind and to both the right and the left of the shine itself were three smaller enclosed structures, each connected to the shrine by smaller walkways and sharing the same sense of design.

He stepped up onto the wooden walkway then stopped, gazing at the Rapture Tree, Blessed of the Goddess. Its trunk was huge, bigger than he could put his arms around, its bark, somewhat pale cream in color, with soft, darker brown stripes tickled around its circumference. Its leaves were oblong in shape, with tips coming to fine points, each one slightly smaller than his palm. Under the tree's grand umbrella swayed vines, stretching in gentle arcs from bough to bough. A couple ends dangled almost touching the ground, their motion in the wind was like that of a sleeping cat's tail.

Quietly, he rolled his duffel off his shoulder and placed it on the floor. His shield and long sword quickly joined the bag, leaning against on the walkway's pillars. Once unloaded from his heavier burdens, he sat down and removed his boots and socks, then placed them next to his other belongings.

He took a moment to let his feet feel the grass below the inner walkway before standing and approaching the Tree. An arm's length from the Tree, he stopped and bowed as gracefully as he could muster, his forehead coming a breath away from touching its trunk.

"Oh Euseeda," he said, his voice low and soft, "I thank thee. I thank thee for the clean water I have drunk, and the rich food upon my table. I thank thee for the children, whose laughter fills

4

my ears, for bountiful harvests, and full tankards that I drink. May you continue to smile upon these lands, and may the people's songs fill your heart. I have come in gratitude for all you have done and provided. Please, allow this humble child to make an offering to you and your Blessed Tree. A piece of myself, a part of my life, so that you, through your favored, may continue to make the land fertile and water sweet."

He stood, bare feet in the soil, his upper arms by his side, elbows bent, and lower arms extended outward, palms up, and face turned to the Great Tree's canopy. Eyes closed, he remained for countless moments, simply existing. And yet, something seemed wrong. He cracked his eyes and peered to one side, then the next, as his body relaxed.

"Where are the Nymphs?" he muttered to himself. "By now they should be practically swarming."

But no one came. The atrium was silent. He backed away from the Tree and took a deep breath.

"Hello?" he boomed loudly, yet without yelling. "Is there anyone here?" his ears strained at the quietness as his voice faded, trying to pick out any sound beyond the leaves and breeze.

A door to the far left building slightly opened. He could almost make out the profile of a man peering from the doorway. Just as quickly as the door opened, it shut again.

Instantly, instinctively, he went from devotee to warrior, his hands drawing his short sword and knife that were still hung from his belt. It only took a few breaths for him to reach the far walkway. Without breaking stride, he leaped up from the atrium's ground, landing to one side of the doorway. Using the tip of his knife, he flicked the door-latch open, then dashed inside, making sure not to stop silhouetted within the door-frame, the short sword held defiantly forward.

At the tip of his blade was a man's throat, muscles trebling. The Adam's apple bounced once as the throat swallowed, veins running its length pulsed for a moment, then disappeared.

But its flesh was a lie.

While it started a pale beige, the color faded into a deep green color, almost brown, as it wrapped around to the back of the neck. Its "skin" was slightly chipped, like bark pulling away from a trunk. Upon the neck was a man's face, long and sharp, with green sideburns disappearing into long, flowing wild hair. Branches stretched out from its hair as if antlers on a stag, yet tiny leaves and small flower buds gave away their true nature. On its brow a knot of wood circled upon itself. Long, goat-like ears that normally flopped to each side of its face had rotated and flared backwards, shaking. Below its throat was a very human torso, arms and hands, well defined, strong, while lanky. All with the same beige coloring in front, then slowly turning to dark green around its backside. Yet, the torso faded within a mane of green only to reappear with the four-legged body of an elk with a large flat tail.

The creature lay frozen on its side, its human torso raised from the ground, its arms stopped in mid-reach towards a now over-boiling pot hanging over a small fire. The dirt pit in floor in which it laid was sunken down, with the cooking hearth in the center. Its emerald eyes were large with surprise, its gaze never wavering from the Warrior's blade.

"Take what you want," it finally muttered, its voice unsteady. "Whatever it is, take it and go."

He knew what this creature was; a sentient plant, a male Dryad, a Keeper of the Blessed Tree of Euseeda. No sooner had his blade started to drop away, the Keeper was gone; bounded away and out the door.

"Ah, crap," he muttered. With well-practiced flourish, the Warrior returned his blades to their scabbards. He grabbed the cloth the Keeper once held and took the boiling pot from the fire. In all the confusion, leaving it there to writhe seemed unwise.

With his hands raised he slowly exited the small room back towards the atrium. He had made a grave error and threatened the holy brother. If he wanted to remain in Euseeda's good graces, he knew he'd have to make amends, somehow.

Fortunately, the Keeper had not gone too far, choosing instead to remain beside his tree. He was partially hidden behind its trunk, one hand resting on the bark, the other in a tight fist. His eyes glared at him with deep intensity, a mix of anger and fear, an animal teetering on the edge of fight or flight.

The Warrior dropped to his knees and bowed deeply on the ground, his own long, braided white hair arching a trail of his body's passage.

"Forgive me, Keeper," he said, his voice muffled slightly, his face pressed into the grass of the atrium's floor. "With the way the door closed I feared burglars were within the shrine."

The air seemed heavy in the silence.

"You reek of salt and brine," the Keeper finally said, never moving from behind his tree. "Why would someone of the sea be here?"

"I am not of the sea," the Warrior replied, never once lifting his head. "I am a follower of Euseeda. I came here to make an offering in her name. Though I did come to this place via the ocean. This is a welcomed break in a modest voyage."

He paused, a thought flickering in his mind.

"Do you have issues with those who tread the waters?" He asked.

"I and my ilk have not had ... fond experiences with those

who ply their skills upon the waves."

"You're talking about the illegal practice of a ship's fawn," The Warrior sat up, swinging his legs around in front and crossing them.

The Keeper nodded, the leaves of his antler-branches dancing slowly.

"I swear upon my real name, I have come with no such foul intention." The Warrior bowed again, his forehead pushed into the earth. "Your Nymphs here are safe."

"How can I trust you?" the Keeper asked, his face stern.

The Warrior sat back up again, but made no motion to return to his feet.

"How can anyone trust anyone else in this world?" He returned.

The Keeper sighed and stepped away from his tree to face

the Warrior. A sad look slowly crossed his face even as their eyes met.

"There are no Nymphs here," he said. "I think in all the time I have been Keeper, I have seen only three come this way. And of those, none have ever returned."

The Warrior looked at the Keeper, surprised. He knew something of Dryads, being a follower of Euseeda. Nymphs, female Dryads, were a gregarious and vivacious lot. When not being struck by wanderlust, they tended to congregate around a Keeper and his Tree. A Keeper without at least a couple of Nymphs was unheard of.

"How do you fare come pollination season without Nymphs?"

"Not easily." The Keeper looked up into his Tree's canopy. "It breaks my heart that the Great Tree has never born fruit, despite all my effort."

"Still, is this place so hard to get to that no Nymph would come?"

The Keeper nodded.

"The only way to Echo Cove is by sea from west. To the east and south our farmland is boxed in by high mountains, and to the north... is the Dead Wood. There is no passage there. If I understand correctly, all the shipping lanes bypass us to travel to one of the great cities farther up the coast. If any boats stop here it's because of bad weather, poor supplies or damage that cannot be patched up enough to limp father along. Most Nymphs travel by road anyway, being fearful and unsteady aboard ship. If they can't pass the Dead Wood, they simply will turn to a simpler and easier destination."

"Bugger," the Warrior grumped as he scratched his soul patch on his chin. "So that's why none appeared when I started the chant for the traditional offering."

"I almost never see a true devotee to Euseeda at this shrine," the Keeper continued, "This place has more ties to Tempest, not his Sister-Wife. So the girls not being here hasn't been that much of a hindrance for the standard offerings the townsfolk occasionally bring. I am sorry that there is no one who can assist with yours."

"Are you saying you can't?"

An awkward silence filled the room.

The Keeper shifted his weight, his tail twitched from side to side for a moment.

"Would you have any issue with my assistance?" He finally asked.

"I'm a sell-sword, a shield for hire. I have traveled too long, waged too many wars, and bled far too often for me to be picky about who helps me with my offerings. I make my offerings to Euseeda wherever I can, whenever I can. For tomorrow, I might not be here to make another."

The Keeper stood there motionless for a moment, slightly biting his lower lip.

"Alright," he said taking a timid step towards the Warrior. "You need to stow your weapons in the storeroom. And you have to take a bath first. There is no way I'm going to allow you to make an offering smelling like you just got worked over by Euseeda's Brother-Husband."

"You have a bath?" the Warrior said, a tiny hint of surprise and longing tinged his voice.

"Weapons. Lockup." The Keeper pointed to the small out building next to his quarters, his voice stern.

The Warrior complied.

The Keeper deftly descended the tree-covered hillside, with clean towels in hand. He had already shown the Warrior to the bath and had given him some alone time before fetching some basic toiletries. The bath itself was more of a small wooden box with a sluice feeding water in from a hot-spring, nestled about one-third way down the hill and hidden within the thick grove, accessible only by the faintest of deer-trails. It was his little secret. One he had now shared with a complete stranger.

The Keeper emerged from the bush and onto the wooden landing the outdoor bath sat upon. There he was, the Warrior, leaning back in the Keeper's private waters.

He was a tall, handsome man. His wet, pale skin gleamed as if made from alabaster in the bright afternoon sunlight that trickled down through the canopy of leaves. Large in the shoulders, yet small in the waist, his body was ripped with carved muscles, yet, his frame was not overbearing and held a sleekness to it. Strong, meaty hands that were bigger than the Keeper's rested gently along the sides of the wooden box. His face was just as finely rendered as his body, long, with a squared jaw offset by an almost delicate nose. Thin, sharp eyebrows rested above his closed small, almond-shaped eyes. With careful grooming, he had nurtured a patch of pale white hair on his chin to form a small, close-cut triangle, broad at the bottom along his jawline, then coming to a sharp point just under his lower lip. He had let his extremely long white hair down from its tight bindings letting it lazily dance across the surface of the warm waters around him, almost hiding his small, pointed ears.

"How should I address you?" the Keeper asked as he stepped forward and placed the towels and toiletries to one side of the tub. "Elf?"

His guest smiled softly for the briefest of moments, before his face returned to a more neutral expression.

"I'm a half-Elf, actually," he said, his sharp, clear amber eyes turning to meet the Keeper's, "On my mother's side. You can call me Warrior. That's what everyone else does. Can I assume, you are fine being addressed as Keeper?"

"As I am the only one here, I see no harm in that," Keeper nodded.

With the air smelling cleaner around Warrior, Keeper was feeling more at ease. Bad memories brought on by the smell of salt and sea had faded once more. It had been a long time since he had someone he could talk to, yet here was this naked half-Elf, sitting in his bath, freely replying to anything he said, providing more information than what was originally asked. He thought for a moment.

"So, you mentioned you were a sell-sword. Does this mean you've traveled the road for a long time?" he finally decided to ask.

On closer inspection, Keeper realized that Warrior was covered in scars of all shapes and sizes, ones that had magic help to heal, leaving but the faintest of color traces on the skin. Though there were three very distinct ones that were more visible than the rest; one on each lower arm running the length from just below his palm to the inside of the elbow, and a single one running down his center of his chest, starting at the clavicle and stopping just shy of his manhood.

Warrior closed his eyes again, leaning back into the waters.

"Nearly as long as I've been alive," he replied.

"Have you ever seen a dragon?" Keeper bent down and

retrieved a hairbrush from the items he had brought.

Warrior sat up in the bath abruptly, warm water spilling over its sides.

"What is it with people and wanting to know about dragons?" he spat. "You let slip even the tiniest mention of having had some sort of possible adventure and the first thing folk ask is if you've seen a dragon?"

"I know," Keeper said, chuckling deeply as he moving around to behind Warrior. "It was a joke."

Warrior glanced at him for a moment, then settled back. He chuckled as well.

"With that jibe, I take it you've seen the long road too?"

"A lifetime ago." Keeper settled himself down next to the bath, the gently reached out and pulled Warrior's hair from the water.

Warrior started to pull away, but Keeper placed his hand on the half-Elf's bare shoulder to stop him.

"You said you wished my assistance," Keeper reminded him.

"For a traditional offering," Warrior said.

"Preparation for such counts as well."

He felt the Warrior relax under his hand.

"Fine. But if I find any flowers in my hair, I'm going to take that brush and shove it up your nose."

Keeper paused. The tone of Warrior's voice told him that the threat was very real. After taking a deep breath, he began carefully brushing the water out of the silver mane.

"Perish the thought."

Keeper fell silent for a few moments as he worked.

"Please," he finally said, "tell me of the world you have seen. It has been ages since I became my Tree's Keeper. I have not left this shrine since. What has happened outside these scared grounds?"

"Humm," Warrior muttered, scratching his little white patch at his chin. "Where to begin?"

"How about your current trip and why you ended up at Echo Cove?"

That soft, timid, off-center smile flashed briefly again at the corners of Warrior's mouth before he started his tale.

Something poked his cheek. Slowly, Warrior became aware of his feet turning cold, but the warmth on his back kept lulling him back into slumber. He felt so relaxed, peaceful and wanted so much to stay that way.

Something poked his cheek again. Begrudgingly, he cracked his eyes. Night had come, turning the entire atrium into hues of blue and dark purple. He was sitting, naked, facing the Great Tree, his legs splayed out before him, his back propped up straight. Around him, his clothes were strewn in the grass and fallen leaves. A knife was standing upwards between his feet. The tip buried in the ground in front of the Great Tree, the last of his blood slipping from its surface. His hair ties had come undone yet again, letting his long snow-white hair dance freely about his face, partially obscuring his vision. He closed his eyes again and rolled his head backwards.

There was that poking again. His vision blurred then came into focus. Keeper's face, a wily smile disguised by tranquil eyes, filled his sight, a single green finger moving out of his vision.

"Crap!" Warrior bolted upright. A sharp pain seared down the center-line of his chest, causing him to buckle farther forward than he'd intended. He hissed. Behind him, he could hear Keeper scramble into all fours.

"Are you okay?" Keeper asked, as he placed a hand on Warrior's back.

Warrior forcibly uncurled himself and looked down his chest. The once bright red line of blood that started at his clavicle and extended past his belly button had turned a deep brown. His lower arms were in similar shape.

"Its fine," he finally hissed, "Just stings like all get-out. Like a bad razor cut from shaving. Look, they're already closing up."

Keeper shook his head, the leaves of his branches rustled.

"I cut too deep," He said while helping Warrior to his feet. "I was afraid something like this would happen."

"Big deal. I've had far worse in battle."

"That's beside the point!" Keeper's front legs pranced, landing heavily in the grass. "I have not preformed the old rites in over a decade. You practically had to walk me though the incantations as it was." He stopped and sighed, turning his face away from Warrior. "I'm sorry."

"Stop your blubbering. You did fine. Especially compared to the last Nymph I had performing those same rites." Warrior bent down to retrieve his underwear. "She nearly chopped my dick in half," he muttered under his breath.

"What?"

Warrior waved the comment away and continued to pick up his clothes. He could feel Keeper's eyes on him as he moved and occasionally hissed when he stretched the wrong way.

"Wait here," Keeper finally said, turned and walked back to his room. He returned a moment later, an amphora in hand. "Face me."

Warrior did as he was told. Keeper cracked the wax seal on

the jar, removing its cork. Tossing the cap aside, he placed the lip to his own. He let the contents flow into his mouth, holding them in his cheeks until they puffed up like a chipmunk's. A golden liquid that smelled of honey, yet moved like water, trickled out the corners and down his chin.

Keeper took a deep breath then forced the liquid from his mouth in a steady stream and onto Warrior's chest, tracing the path of the cut until his cheeks were empty. Warrior winced. Then Keeper closed his eyes and reached out with his fingers to trace the wound. As he did so, the sharpness of the cut subsided, the bleeding disappeared, leaving healthy skin in its place.

"Ah," Warrior said as he felt the wounds wash away, "See, you do remember some of your rituals."

Keeper snorted.

"Arm," he said as he slapped Warrior's elbow. Warrior raised him arms, one after the other to have the same healing done to them. Once Keeper was done, he placed the amphora aside and helped Warrior with retrieving the rest of his clothes.

"Where shall you go from here?" Keeper asked as he handed a belt to Warrior.

"Probably back to my bunk on the ship," Warrior replied as he slipped the knife back into its scabbard. "It took a lot longer to get up here than I had planned and I don't want to miss the outgoing tide." He offered the sheathed knife back to Keeper, who took it.

Warrior turned and walked to the storehouse to retrieve the rest of his gear. It took him no time at all to re-armor and arm himself. Once he had put his boots on, he did not reenter the atrium proper, instead stood on the walkway surrounding the Great Tree. After slipping the leather strap that held his huge scutum shield in place across his back, he hefted his duffel bag over it. He turned back to Keeper.

There was a silence the filled the shrine, thick and palatable. The two stood for a time, Warrior slightly turned to Keeper. It seemed like there was something Keeper wanted to say, and Warrior stood, waiting for it to be said.

"All right," were the words Keeper finally uttered. "Be careful going down the steps, the fog rolls in here early and does not burn off until well past sunrise."

Warrior nodded and stepped away from the walkway. He got half way across the courtyard before stopping.

"Are you lonely?" he asked over his shoulder.

Keeper took a while to answer.

"I have my Tree, and I have Euseeda. That is all that I need."

Warrior began to walk into the darkness.

"However," Keeper added, his voice timid, "If you pass this way again, please take more time to visit. I would like to hear stories of your travels."

Before descending the stairs, Warrior raised his hand waving it slightly back and forth, the polished metal of his gauntlet catching the moonlight.

His little shore-leave was over. At least he had made a friend.

And in this world, he needed all the friends he could get.

The Keeper's Tree

It was a full five years since he had first laid eyes on the small village of Echo Cove. Yet not much had changed. The small harbor was still deep, the single wooden pier under his plate boots stood strong against the rhythmic waves. The town still crawled up the cliff-side with windy stone streets. And the shrine was still visible just over the cliff-edge to the east. The morning mist had finally been burned away, leaving the air clean and colors sharp.

This time, the Warrior had planned his trip to such an isolated community better. He had found a trading ship that actually did regular calls to this port bringing in wine, cloth, and metal that the village could not provide for itself. As such, the call would be much longer than his original visitation, a good week before the trading and bartering was done and the ship was ready to leave for the next destination.

Iron clad, sword scabbards at his hips, shield and duffel on his back, he made his way up the streets to the Shrine of Euseeda above. Being a fine, late spring day, he saw more people than his first visit. Shops were open and people cheerfully ran about their daily business. The smell of fresh baked goods wafted down alleys making his belly grumble. Finally he gave in and stopped in one of the corner bakeries along his way to buy some bread, enough for three meals and a snack.

While munching on a small, round roll, he eventually made his way up to the shrine. The stairs, unfortunately were as steep as he remembered. As he climbed, the sound and smells of the town slowly faded away, to be replaced by gentle winds rustling through new green leaves, and the smell of sap and bark. The shade of the tree-lined path broke at the top, letting the warm sunlight caress his pale cheeks. The grass-covered courtyard stretched before him, better manicured than any palace ground, the hewn stonework set into the earth marked the traveled path to the shrine itself.

"Well," came a deep and pleasant voice off to his right. "I did not expect to see you here again."

The Warrior turned towards the voice. The shrine's Keeper bore a wide, friendly smile that shone from under the shade of the wide-brimmed sun-hat he wore precariously between his antler-branches. His chest was covered with a thick leather bib that tied around his waist and stretched down to his front knees. His gloved hands held a large pair of heavy shears. Across his withers hung two very large canvas bags, filled with bush trimmings.

"Yard-work?" Warrior asked.

"Someone has to," Keeper laughed as he walked over, his four cloven hooves barely making any sound at all on the grass. He paused for a moment, closed his eyes, then took the longest and deepest breath of any creature Warrior had ever seen.

"I smell... baked goodies."

"Good nose." Warrior replied. "I've brought a common offering this time."

"And good timing you have," said Keeper, placing his cutting shears into one of the sacks. "Come, join me for lunch."

Keeper led Warrior to the shrine proper. Instead of

stepping onto the walkway that encircled the Great Tree, Keeper nimbly hopped over and into the atrium proper. As for himself, Warrior stopped on the wood flooring. He rolled his duffel and shield off his back, unbuckled his sword belt, then sat on the edge and removed his plate boots and socks. Before standing up, he reached over and opened his bag then produced some of the bread he had bought. He took the largest of the loaves, a braided affair that had been glazed and sprinkled with small, white flower-seeds, and extended it to Keeper.

Keeper simply smiled and motioned to the offering box at the roots of the Great Tree.

Warrior rose and walked over to the box. It was no more than a foot across and two feet wide, sunk into the ground, little more than a metal lip and simple copper cover with a finger hole on its left side. He bowed before the tree, presenting the bread in his hands. He then knelt down and lifted the lid. Inside, the four walls and bottom of the box were made completely from tangled, tightly woven roots.

"Are you sure?" he asked Keeper. "Should you not be presenting this to your tree yourself?"

Keeper came to stand alongside the tree, one hand resting on its pale trunk.

"This is a small shrine, not a big temple," Keeper replied. "We have no need of tight observance of formalities. The offering itself is the important part, not how it was offered."

He paused for a moment, his green eyes, resting up on the center of the tree's canopy. A long, flopped ear twitched slightly, then calmed. Keeper's gaze returned to the Warrior.

"He also likes to know the people who give him offerings. So few do that he cherishes each and every one."

Warrior cocked an eyebrow. "He?"

Keeper nodded. "'He' in the loosest, most generic sense of the word."

"I thought the correct term was 'She'."

Deep rumblings of laughter boomed throughout the atrium. "Ah, you really are a devotee of the Goddess, to know that. You are correct, for the most part. Rapture Trees are both male and female. But he has always struck me more male, than female in character, so in my own mind, it's 'He'."

Warrior nodded. "A good a reason as any."

"Now," Keeper said, "place your offering in the box. Before you cover it back up, take your hand and touch one of the box's sides and speak whatever you want to say to him."

Warrior did as he was told, barely fitting the loaf into the box. He then rested his palm against the closest box wall. It was surprisingly warm to the touch. He could feel the roots of the Great Tree shift slightly, a rhythmic sensation, like one taking a slow but shallow breath. It surprised him a little. He had never touched a tree before, let alone its delicate roots. But his hand remained steady.

"Enjoy," he finally said before removing his hand and replacing the lid.

"Is that all?" Keeper asked, a bemused smile lighting up his sharp features.

"What else is there to say?" Warrior replied as he rose to his feet. Under him, he could faintly make out the sensation of the ground stirring, moving, despite the topsoil never being disturbed.

"Normally, folks give their thanks for all the good he has done for them, in the name of Euseeda," Keeper said as he stepped next to the Warrior.

"That's for later. For a more traditional offering." Warrior looked at his hand, his own fingers tracing the sensation of the Tree's warmth across his palm. "I feel like I have been blessed."

"That's because you have been. He has not forgotten the offering you made of yourself the last time you came here."

"You can really hear the Tree, can't you?" Warrior's eyes looked up to meet Keeper's.

Keeper turned and started to walk towards the small room in the back of the shrine. "I don't know if 'hear' is the proper word..," he replied over his shoulder, "it's more like 'feel', or 'sense'. I thought you of all folk would have known that, given the previous knowledge you've displayed about the worship of Euseeda."

Warrior bowed once again to the Tree, gathered his things, then quickly followed. "Not many Keepers have been forthcoming on their relationship with their trees."

Keeper sighed. "You are probably right on that. Despite the fact that my kind need and desire to be with all the folk of the world, it always feels like a wall is there. You and your kin know little of my kin, yet the same can be said in reverse." He opened the door to his living chamber and motioned for Warrior to enter.

The room was just as Warrior remembered, solid wood floor, with a hole in the middle that dropped down to a cooking hearth. One side of the room was lined with chests and cabinets containing a selection of utensils and dry goods. There also sat a rack of small, corked amphorae, in a dark corner. On the opposite side, lay a pile of straw neatly arranged to form a bed, with a single sheet spread over the top, and a well-loved blanket curled at its feet. There were two cushions resting near the edge of the flooring before the center pit. Beyond that, there were no chairs, or tapestries. No mirrors, no scrolls, not even an icon of Euseeda herself. Nothing but the barest of essentials.

After depositing his armored boots, shield and weapons to the left of the doorway, Warrior unceremoniously plopped down on one of the cushions, letting his bare feet touch the dirt floor below. He opened his bag again and produced the rest of the bread rolls.

"Eh, people are people wherever you go," he said as he closed the duffel and pushed it back towards the rest of his possessions. He watched as Keeper removed his gloves, the silly sun-hat, and the two sacks full of leaves and branches from his withers.

"On an individual character basis, I could not agree with you more." Keeper retrieved a pair of plates and cups from his cupboard, then looped a single finger into an amphora and raised it from its rack.

"However, I also fully understand that my kind's instinctual needs do not mesh well with your kin's cultural ideals. Before becoming my tree's keeper, I saw way too many Nymphs go to great pains to hide the fact that they were not of blood and bone. I think that is where the wall comes from."

Keeper handed a plate and cup to Warrior. He removed the amphora's cork with his teeth, then offered its contents to his guest. Warrior raised his cup to catch the amber liquid. While it moved like water, it smelled of sweet sap and honey, with a bright nearly glowing golden color.

"Holy wine?" Warrior asked, looking deep into his cup.

"It's wine. It's meant to be drunk. I make far too much to ever use for religious ceremonies. I don't think anyone would fault me for sharing a bit with company."

Warrior snorted, yet the corner of his mouth tipped up into a soft smile, then disappeared as quickly as it came. He handed Keeper a roll.

The wine was truly the sweetest drink he had ever tasted, yet was not cloying to the palate. The alcohol content was very low, making him wonder if he drank this all day, would he ever feel a buzz; but it meshed surprisingly well with the fresh bread.

"You know," Warrior finally said after washing down another bite of his roll. "That wall will always be there if you keep cloistered up here on your hill."

Keeper looked up from his cup, his eyes wide, one of his eyebrows cocked, his ears held slightly higher than normal.

"How many people know that you're here?" Warrior continued, "I bet the whole town knows the shrine is here. Hells, you can see it from the harbor. But that doesn't mean they know YOU are here."

Keeper's deep green tail twitched nervously from side to side.

"There are three, maybe four," he replied after a long moment. "I tend not to involve myself in offerings unless asked."

Warrior kneaded his forehead with one hand. "You were hiding back here the first time I came, weren't you?"

"Um, yes."

"Yet you came and greeted me today," Warrior sighed, "despite the fact that I have not been here in what, nearly five years?"

Keeper placed his plate on the floor, then crossed his arms in front of his chest, making his leather apron buckle. He cocked his head to one side, his eyes closed.

"I'm... really not sure why," he said straightening himself again. "Maybe... Maybe it's because, the first time I met you, you seemed to have a kindred spirit about you."

"You seem pretty damned lonely up here, despite your claims to the contrary."

"I have learned over the years to be content with what life has given me," Keeper replied. "I'm afraid I am not as brave as you to... rock the boat."

Warrior tossed the last piece of his roll into his mouth, then washed it down with his wine.

"Bravery, is not something you have or not have. It's the realization that being afraid won't save your ass."

"Spoken like someone who has seen the oliphaunt," Keeper chuckled, a sound so deep that it was barely audible but could be felt through the floorboards.

The Warrior placed his empty cup into the center of his crumb lined plate. "You seem of good folk, Keeper. I think..." He paused, his lips scrunched up to one side. "Bah, it's your choice. I've said my peace."

"And I thank you for your concern," Keeper bowed his head towards Warrior. "I suppose you have to hurry on your way again?"

Warrior shook his head. "I have a few days before I have to ship off."

"I see. You're simply passing through then?"

"No," Warrior said, "I came here specifically. I ... needed some quiet time, to get my head straight. And this harbor town seemed like the place to do just that."

"There's something troubling you?" Keeper asked.

Warrior pursed his lips for just a moment, but said nothing.

"Can you talk about it?"

Warrior looked away from Keeper. "No."

After a long silence, Warrior stood and stretched his arms.

"I suppose I should go find an inn for the next couple of nights."

Keeper picked up the used plates, took Warrior's cup and sat it on the floor beside the seat cushion, then rose himself to his hooves. He deposited what he held into a large metal pail, presumably to be taken outside later and washed. Then he refilled the lone cup.

"If you don't mind sleeping in the girl's quarters, there is more than enough room here, if you wish."

"Wouldn't the Nymphs mi..." Warrior paused. "Oh, right. No Nymphs." He bent down to retrieve the now-full wine cup and drew another long drink.

"I don't need much, just a place outta the weather I can flop a bedroll down."

"I think that can be arranged," Keeper said. "Please, feel free to come and go as you like. In the meantime, let me excuse myself to make sure the room is clean and ready for you." He nodded once, the leaves of his rack bobbing in sync. Then he turned and left the room, leaving the door open behind him.

Warrior watched Keeper with bemusement as he walked to the far side of the atrium his tail ticking from side to side in counterpoint to the movement of his rear legs. It probably would not have grabbed Warrior's attention like it did except for the tail and backside being such a dark green standing out against Keeper's big, cream colored spot that covered his entire rear-end. He chuckled quietly to himself before taking another drink.

After a while, he stepped from the room until his feet were once again on the atrium grass. He sat down on the walkway, facing the Great Tree, his elbows on his knees, back slumped, and his nearly empty cup floating between his fingertips.

"You have a good Keeper," he said. "He seems wise, yet innocent. Shy yet trusting."

He closed his eyes. The calm sounds of the hilltop tickled at his small, pointed ears. This place was so soothing to him, he had almost forgotten the trouble he was in. At least until Keeper had brought it up. He breathed deep, letting his mind empty out and just listened to the wind in the Great Tree's leaves.

80   03

He was falling.
Deep.
Down.
To places unseen.
Blackness no torch could light.
Mine!
The voice was gut wrenching, more feeling than sound.
Claws across wood, rending flesh.
You are MINE! The world is MINE!

Warrior jerked himself up, his eyes wide, his mind full awake, racing. Forcibly, he calmed himself again. He bent over, placing his head in his right hand, while the other still dangled his cup. Under his feet, he could subtly feel the earth move.

He raised his head again to look at the Great Tree. The nightmare was calling him again. He knew he had to do something about it, and soon. But he had no idea what. He finished off the last of his cup, all the while wishing it was something stronger.

He placed the cup on the walkway, then turned and bowed to the Tree.

"I'm sorry to have troubled you," he said.

With that, he left, still barefoot, to find himself a drink that would knock him under the table.

It was nearly the witching hour before he returned, staggering. He oh so didn't want to climb those Hells' damned stairs. Even more so now that there were three sets of them, spinning. Flopping onto the stone steps, his mind numb, he began his ascent on his hands and knees. At the top, he rolled over onto his back-plate and waited for the world to stop.

A shadow crossed the moonlight. He squinted, trying to make the shape out.

"Where have you been?"

"Drinkin'." Warrior smiled sloppily at Keeper.

"I can smell that." The stag-man waved a hand in front of his face. "Thrushweaver's been having fits since you left." He bent down and hauled Warrior up.

"Thush-weavah?" Warrior asked as he leaned into

Keeper's torso.

Keeper gave him a long hard glance before starting to walk forward. "You're too drunk to remember even if I told you."

"You say that like it'sh a bad thin'."

Keeper rolled his eyes.

"Ya know, there'sh a tavern by tha docksh, the Shword and Board. Hash shome wonderfully nashty sshit. You should try there shome time."

"I think you've drunk enough for the both of us," Keeper replied, his head craning to avoid Warrior's breath.

As they walked, Warrior stumbled, nearly dragging Keeper down.

"Euseeda! Could you have not at least taken off your armor before going on a drinking binge?"

Warrior thumbed his breastplate. "Ish light. Ish shecond shkin. Only 70'ish poundsh."

"I fear your definition of 'light' and mine might differ." Keeper kept walking, dragging Warrior with him. "Let's get you to bed."

The Warrior forced himself up, despite the fact that the grass growing outside was too loud. The sun had already broken the night's veneer and was peeking through the tree tops and into the window. Sitting up in the straw bed, he clutched his head in his hands. It took all his willpower not to toss the remnants of last night's food and drink. It had been a long time since he had a hangover this mighty. He needed water. And the hair of the dog that bit him.

He peered through his barely open eyes to find a pitcher, sitting neatly on the floor nearby inside of a small wash basin.

There was a cup next to it, as well as two neatly rolled washcloths and a towel. Ignoring the cup, he snatched the pitcher from its rest, pressed its spout to his lips, opened his throat wide and guzzled its entire contents. The cool water leaked out the sides of his mouth in great torrents, running down his square jawline, danced across his bobbing Adam's apple then dripped down his chest. After replacing the pitcher, he waited on the edge of the straw bedding.

It took several minutes, but the sound of the butterfly's flapping outside softened, and his gut calmed. Fully opening his eyes, he took a survey of his surroundings.

He seemed to be back at the shrine. The room, itself, was much larger than Keeper's quarters, yet looked almost exactly alike, minus the cooking hearth and other sundry furniture. Instead, in the center was the straw bedding that he sat upon, a simple white sheet covering it to keep the shafts from poking into his skin. A well-worn but clean wool blanket had been pulled over him.

Near the foot of his bedding, stood a single clothes rack. A solid post rose from three legs, only to have another wooden bar, smoothly shaped like a lady's collarbone, cross near its top. It was well worn, but richly painted with delicate flowers and vines. Obviously intended to display a woman's fine dress.

Now, however, it held Warrior's armor, properly layered; padding, chain, then the plate chest, with the shoulder guards buckled underneath. His chain pants and greaves dangled from below, but did not touch the ground. From behind the stand, he could barely see his shield and sword belt peeking over the shoulders. To the right, was his duffel bag, to the left, his plate boots and gauntlets, with his shift, pants, socks and braies laid out in front.

He paused, his hand tugging at his shirt. He looked down to find himself wearing a smock that was not his own. Its linen was slightly yellower than what he preferred, red embroidery gathered into artistic pleats across his breast, and it hung to his knees. Its wrists were gathered in the same smocking gathers. But beyond that, there was nothing else.

His long, waist length white hair had been undone from its normal high bound ponytail and spread across his shoulders, covering his eyes. Idly, he ran his fingers through it. There was not nearly as many knots as it should have had for going to bed with it unbrushed. Someone had taken care of it, of him.

He put his head back into his hands, his elbows onto his knees. He had no clue how he got here. He could not remember leaving the tavern. Hells, he could barely remember going to the tavern. He flopped back into the straw.

"Whatever I had last night must have been really bad," he muttered to himself. "Or really, really good."

He mustered his will and got out of bed. Morning drills were calling him. He knew from long experience that skipping them, even when ill, could mean the difference of life or death on the long road. With his sword-belt around his waist, he left the room and made his way to the courtyard.

Despite his still throbbing head, he began, slowly with his longsword in hand, then picked up steam as his body took over from his conscious mind. In no time at all, he had worked up a sweat with basic thrusts and slashes. His shortsword joined his long in the dance of movement, spinning and flashing in the morning light. His breath synced with his movements, the whistling through his teeth as he exhaled creating a sing-song note-less tone.

"You're up earlier than I expected." The deep voice came

from his right, in the direction of the main shrine.

"I overslept," he replied, not breaking his movements, never once looking at Keeper.

"Please, what troubles you?"

Warrior stomped the ground with his bare foot as he thrust his longsword forward at an imaginary shadow.

"What makes you think I'm troubled?"

"The Great Tree was having fits of worry when you left yesterday. I must assume he sensed something amiss from you."

Warrior stopped in mid-move, his balance precarious yet stable. His head turned slightly to bring Keeper inside his view.

"Thrushweaver?"

"So you do remember something of last night," Keeper said, crossing his arms in front of his chest. "I miss-spoke his true name in my worry. Better to you than someone else, I suppose."

"I did not know the Trees had names," Warrior replied returning to his drills.

He could here Keeper sigh behind him.

"Most forget their names," Keeper replied. "I only think his name is Thrushweaver. But he seems happy with it so that is what I call him."

"You think?"

"Remember, they can't speak in words. Not like you and I. Only images and emotions." Keeper's voice seemed inordinately sad. "When I first became his Keeper, he showed me an image of a small brown-black woodland bird, holding a thread in its beak and dancing between the strands of a loom, like a shuttlecock."

"Yeah, that sounds like a 'Thrushweaver'." Warrior's blades continued to slice the air around him, crossing in front of his body, making the wind move his hair.

"I have answered your question, now answer mine."

Warrior finished with a final big sweep, then returned his swords to their sheaths. He stood silently for a time, his face dripped with perspiration, his hands resting on the pommels of each blade. He closed his eyes and steadied his breathing.

"If your Tree was truly worried, then maybe this would be best said in front of him."

Keeper nodded and extended an arm as if opening a pathway for Warrior to enter the shrine itself. Warrior walked past him, and moved into the atrium, and faced Thrushweaver. Keeper followed coming to rest besides the half-Elf.

After a long, tense moment, Warrior took a deep breath.

"I have made a mistake," he finally said, his voice cracking slightly. "A big one. And I fear that all the known lands are going to pay the price for my folly."

Keeper placed a hand on Warrior's shoulder.

"What happened?"

Warrior looked at his feet.

"Have you ever dealt with the undead?"

Exploring the catacombs had gone on for days. Warrior and his companions had been hired two weeks ago to explore the forgotten ruins by the city mayor when construction of a new bathhouse had unearthed them. It sounded like an easy job. Go in with a team that he knew well, do a basic mapping to see how extensive these stone covered tunnels ran, and clear out any unwanteds. And for the most part it had gone smoothly enough.

But being in the dank darkness was starting to wear on his team's nerves. The Magician of the Arcane Tower and the Holy Knight of Luran were bickering about turning around. The Priest of Tempest wore an even more bored expression than normal.

Even his most faithful partner, the Ranger, Weapons Mistress and Animal Handler, was getting fidgety about being underground for so long, her fox was constantly twitching and yipping at false shadows. Yet they had not found the end of the catacombs.

Under the flicker of torchlight, Warrior kept pressing on, hoping to find a small sliver of dry land and get his feet out of the murk. Alas, no such place was presenting itself. He stopped when he felt a hand on his shoulder.

"Please, we've got to turn around," Ranger said.

He turned to face her, the torch held to one-side so as not be in either of their direct vision. Taller than he was, with long wavy red-brown hair, she held a fierce wildness to her. Clad in a full leather girdle and bristling with weapons of all ilk, very few could go toe to toe with her. Including himself.

"While I've done my best to keep a map of where we've gone, we're on the ragged edge of being permanently lost," She continued. "We've done what we came to do. Let's get out, report in, find us an inn to dry off and call this job done."

"Oh so done," Magician added, wringing out the bottom of his robe for the umpteenth time.

"Yeah, there's nothing here," said Holy Knight. "Short of the all the corpses. And they aren't moving anytime soon."

The Priest yawned.

"I know you like to leave no stone unturned," Ranger continued, "but I really don't think we'll find anything but more of the same. You know all that'll happen is that they will board this place up, sealing it, and toss our hard-made map into an archive to be forgotten again."

As she talked, Warrior glanced over her shoulder. The far wall didn't look right. It was subtle, nearly imperceptible in the dim dancing light. He walked over, looking the stonework up and down. While the archway implanted in the wall was nothing new, the entire length of the winding tunnels had been a running motif of them, the stonework was not consistent with its neighbors. One swift kick, and it all came down reveling a small recess with a bound stone chest.

"Great..." Holy Knight threw up her hands and turned in place, the chain under her surcoat ringing in the darkness as she moved. "Leave it to the meat-shield to find the hidden chest. I thought that was your job," she said turning to Ranger.

Ranger snorted. "It's our Warrior who learned a couple of thief skills. Not I. I just draw maps."

"I don't think my knack for disarming traps counts towards kicking in stone walls with rotted mortar," Warrior replied.

Priest craned his head around the now open space. "Anything we need to kill in there?"

"Doesn't look it," Warrior said.

"Meh." Priest turned away to lean against the far wall.

Magician came forward and stood behind the girls. "Well, open it. Let's see what we've got."

As typical, Warrior had been 'volunteered'. First to open, and first to get smacked in the face with any trap it might conceal. He took a moment to sling his giant shield around his back in an effort to free his hands. After everyone else in the party took a step back, he knelt to examine the chest more closely.

It was more of a small sarcophagus than a chest, hinged with thick iron, but no lock. There was no marking or decoration, just rough-hewn rock, the same stone that the rest of the catacombs were made of. After doing another check around all sides, he passed the torch back to Magician.

The lid, at first, did not want to budge. But with tenacity

and a prayer to Euseeda the mortar holding it in place cracked and gave way. For a moment the air dropped a degree or two making the hair on the back of his neck rise. He motioned for the torch to be passed back.

Inside, the chest was empty, save for a few blue shards of broken crystal glass at the bottom.

"Hells," he muttered. "Someone's beat us here." He could hear the team groan behind him. He reached into the chest and pulled a small sliver out. He turned it under the torch, the light rippled through the glass, casting eerie blue colors on the walls around them. While somewhat pretty, it was, effectively, junk. He tossed it back into the chest.

He rose and turned to his team. "Come on, let's go."

Ranger slapped him on the back. "Don't worry. Our next job will be more adventurous."

"That's what I'm afraid of."

"And hopefully," Magician added, "Less damp."

I wouldn't count on it.

Instantly the party jumped to the ready, weapons drawn, Warrior, Knight, and Ranger encircling the Priest and Magician. For a moment, all that any of them could hear was each other. Gloved hands shifting against leather grips, breaths strong and harsh, cloth shifting and water disturbed.

In the darkness came a faint rattle. Nerves tightened it became louder and louder. And into the light, stepped a skeleton, an undead, bathed in blue fire.

Then another.

And another.

The sound of bone on stone echoed, louder and louder.

"RUN!" Warrior cried. He did not need to yell it twice. His companions had already started to move. Turning on his heels, he charged down the passageway from whence they came.

Undead boiled out of every crack and crevice, hands grasping, clawing doing everything in their power to pull the party under the mass of bone and rotten flesh. Warrior put his full weight behind his scutum shield, plowing a path through the human carcasses, ethereal blue flames licking around the edges. Behind him he could hear the crushing sounds of Knight's giant two-handed mace, splintering bone. Bolts of blue whizzed past his head, helping clear his next foothold, all the while the soft drone from the Priest energized him. As they moved, with torch in hand, Ranger announced each and every turn.

It took hours to fight their way past the mobs of the unliving. And another day to reach the sunlight, never once stopping for rest. Warrior collapsed on the dirt of the construction site. He was so tired and ached so much it took what little will he had left to not dry-heave. He did not need to look to know his team was in no better shape.

Around them workers milled. Warrior's head was spinning so much he could not make out a word they said.

"Seal it," he said weakly, his lungs still gasping for breath, his hand pointing to the unearthed entrance. "Get the biggest rock you can and seal it."

The workers milled nervously.

"NOW!" he bellowed, his own voice threatened to split his skull in two. Instantly, someone started barking orders and the workers were off. It did not take them long to find a block big enough to close it off.

Knight was the first to recover enough to sit up. "Praise Luran, skeletons can't run. We'd be dead else-wise."

"That was fun!"

The entire party glared at Priest.

Warrior turned his head slightly, his gaze falling on the Magician. "That... voice we heard. Do you think?"

"No thinking about it," Magician's white brow furrowed. "We woke up a Liche."

A Foreman walked up to the party, grapevine staff in hand.

"It's sealed." he said bluntly. "Anything else?"

"Yes," Knight replied. "Go to the city's biggest temple and get the highest ranking cleric possible. That stone must be bound, not just by weight, but by divine powers."

"That's not going to hold him for long, if it really is a Liche," Priest said.

Magician nodded.

"True, but I hope it'll hold him until we can figure out our next move."

"We're not strong enough." Warrior closed his eyes. "We

need an army to take on a Liche."

Ranger sat up and took her fox into her arms, holding it close to hide her shaking. "We need a miracle."

⁓ ◌

"After the escape, it didn't take us long to figure out 'who' we woke up," Warrior said. "Hurraden the Eternal."

Keeper crossed his arms in front of his chest, his head tilted to the right as he listened. He had sat there nearly motionless, his big rump on the grass, while his front legs propped him up to nearly his full height.

"The King who would be God?" he asked, his gem-like eyes focued on Warrior.

Warrior nodded.

"A week after we fled the crypt, the sealing stone cracked and his army spewed forth. It completely overran the city, claiming more bodies for its horde as it went." Warrior's eyes looked away from Keeper. "Euseeda, what a mess."

"Where are your companions now?" Keeper's front legs bent and he lowered his elk-belly onto the grass.

"We split up." Warrior replied. "The others went to various places to see if we could round up allies to help in this fight. I came here to clear my head to think of a strategy against it all. The undead we can eventually win against, with enough manpower and holy magics. But Hurraden's sorcery is fueling them... Unless we are rid of him, they will keep coming, infinitum."

"I must say, I am impressed at your bravery," Keeper said. "With the picture you have painted, I'd have thought nothing less of you if you and your team had turned tail and ran."

"We... I made this mess. I was the one who woke him up. I have to stop it. I don't have a choice."

Keeper ran a finger along the base of his right ear. "But from your description, there was no phylactery. Liche souls are bound to one. Or did I miss something?"

"It was there, just not whole. And I didn't realize it at the time."

Keeper's brow furrowed. "The blue shards?"

Warrior nodded.

Keeper was suddenly on his four hooves, his eyes wide, his fingers splayed out from his palms. "You touched his phylactery?"

Warrior buried his face into his hands, his elbows burrowing into his knees. He heard Keeper bound away.

He did not blame him. He knew it was only a matter of time before the Liche came to claim his body for its own. The more he thought about it the more afraid he became. And with the fear, came the darkness, welling, churning from deep inside. He tried to steady his mind, his will and resolve being the only things keeping the darkness from swallowing him whole.

A strong hand grabbed his hair by the brow and jerked his head upwards. Keeper was back, a leather bag hung around his neck, a drinking cup full of holy wine in his other hand. His face was stern, his eyes dilated so that only the thinnest of green lines encircled giant black orbs and in his mouth was one of Thrushweaver's vines as if sucking on the end of a rope.

Keeper splashed the entire cup of wine into Warrior's face. Warrior tried to pull away, his eyes stinging, but Keeper's hold on his brow remained firm. Keeper dropped the empty cup, only to replace it with a small, thick, flat glass jar from the bag. Using his pinky and ring fingers, he pressed the jar into his palm, popped its lid off which his thumbnail, then plunged his thumb tip inside. When his thumb reappeared it was covered in a fine golden dust.

41

Holding Warrior's head still, Keeper pressed the dust into the half-Elf's forehead. A deep resonating hum softly throbbed against the soles of Warrior's feet. It took a moment for him to realize it was Keeper making the sound. As Keeper's wordless voice continued, he shifted Warrior's head from side to side, his dust laden thumb traced marks across Warrior's brow then slowly down his face. Stroke by stroke, Warrior felt the darkness subside, pushed farther back than his own will could ever achieve. He closed his eyes and forced himself to relax, trusting completely in Keeper's touch.

Half an hour later, Keeper loosened his grip on Warrior's hair. Stumbling, Keeper stepped back then collapsed onto the atrium's floor, the Great Tree's vine falling from his mouth. His form twisted oddly on the soil; his elk body lay on its side, yet his human torso craned so that it faced skywards, only to have his head turned to opposite direction by his branches, forcing the side of his face into the earth. Both sets of lungs heaved in unison, gasping for breath.

Around Warrior the world came into sharper focus, brighter than it had been for many days. The sun felt warmer, the late morning breeze like a long lost lover's caress. Just beneath the surface of his skin, he could just barely detect the tingly glow of the signs that had been woven. His headache was gone along with the sinking pit in his gut. He took a deep breath, reveling in the air's sweetness.

"What did you do?" Warrior finally asked.

"Those wards should buy you time," Keeper finally replied, still stretched prone beneath his tree. His voice was harsh and cracked. "Not a true banishment, but a barrier. A temporary one at that."

"I thought you said you don't know most of the rituals of

Euseeda." Warrior rose and walked over to Keeper. He knelt down, his weight balanced on his toes, his knees splayed, his head casting a shadow across Keeper's face.

"I don't." Keeper closed his eyes. "But Thrushweaver remembers."

Warrior turned and faced the Great Tree. Dropping his knees into the grass, he bowed until his head touched the soil.

"Thank you," he said, his voice soft.

A moment later he stood and gazed upon the Tree. Warrior's brow furrowed.

"How much does he remember? That was no simple blessing you just cast. I have only felt holy magic like that from an arch-bishop."

Keeper raised a hand towards Warrior. He took it and pulled Keeper upright so that the stag-man now rested on his stomach, his four legs folded under him.

"Thrushweaver is more of a god than that Liche could ever hope to be," Keeper said. "Even I don't know the extent of my Tree's power. Though I suppose you could say that of all Rapture Trees. They are, after all, extensions of the Goddess herself."

Warrior sat down in the grass facing Keeper. He scratched his chin right where his soul patch rested, his eyes flickering this way and that, yet never actually looking at anything.

"Trees purify the land and water..." he muttered to himself. "I suppose there is no way in all the Hells I can convince you to come with me, in Thrushweaver's name."

"Ha ha ha ha – No."

"Right." Warrior continued to scratch at his chin. "Would it be possible to get a series of wards, like the ones that were placed on me, then? And if so, what do you and Thrushweaver ask in return?"

Keeper's ear twitched and his gaze turned away from Warrior to his Tree. A long silence hung in the atrium as a conversation took place that no one could hear.

Warrior waited.

"That's hard to say," Keeper finally replied, without looking away from his Tree. "We have little use for gold or riches. And the few townsfolk who do worship here bring enough offerings that we want for little else."

He crossed his arms in front of his chest and cocked his head to one side. "I suppose we can start with traditional morning and evening devotionals for the remainder of your stay. Without the bloodletting. We don't want to break those wards already spun. And no more getting wasted drunk. I do NOT want to haul your armored butt across that courtyard again."

"Right."

Keeper stood, raising first his front half, then his back. "Sounds like we have work to do. I assume you have a plan on what you want done?"

"Still working it out," Warrior said as he too stood. "You should rest a bit first. You look exhausted after that weaving."

"No. It is not yet noon. Your morning devotional first." Keeper said. "Then I shall nap. And you shall go prepare us a hearty lunch. I think we shall need it."

Warrior nodded then removed his wine-stained smock. He had agreed and while the sun was high, it had not yet climbed overhead. It was a bit of splitting hairs on Keeper's part, but he was not about to complain. This, in the end, was a pittance compared to what he asked for. And he knew it.

It had taken nearly a week for the two to gather all the

materials needed and spin the wards required. They had started with his armor, etching the holy symbols on the inside of each plate piece. Protecting himself from the undead's necromantic magics was his first goal. They then created a series of small vials filled with holy wine with a single wood chit, a rune inscribed within. The vials made for excellent little anti-undead-bombs. They were followed by wooden talismans made from Thrushweaver's own bark with a simple leather lanyard, as many of them as they could muster. He did not know how many were going to be involved in this fight, and he felt that he needed to extend Euseeda's protection to as many as he could. That left only one object to make, and only a day to do it in.

Warrior made his way back towards the docks. He had remembered that the first time he had come here, Keeper had mentioned that the townsfolk were more tied to Tempest than Euseeda. If that were true, then the Cove should also have a temple to Tempest as well. But he did not remember seeing any such place in his brief travels to the port town before. If anyone could tell him where the temple was, it would be those folk who make their living at sea.

It didn't take long to be pointed in the right way. According to the directions he got, there were two paths to the temple. The main way was indeed through the town on the upper levels and ran down the west side of the ridge-line farther past where he had explored. There was, however another path from the pier, that ran close to the shoreline and around the edge of the bay. It was smaller, just wide enough for foot traffic, and one could easily lose their footing due to the wet stone.

He rounded the edge of the harbor to be greeted by a low garden maze of tide pools. The walkway split and wound through the tiny ponds and he had to take careful steps to make sure he did not tread on any sea-life trying to cross from one to another. At the far end an archway of coral rose, sculpted into two giant waves cresting its top and meeting in the middle at the symbol of Tempest; a crab wielding a trident. Behind the arch, he could see the temple proper, a great Parthenon that opened to the sea.

Warrior stopped before the archway. Looking to the right, he found a simple rope cord that passed through the stonework and pulled it. To one side, he could hear a ship's bell distinctive clang. He waited.

It was some time before a young lady came to the archway. She must have been a good head smaller than he, with flowing blonde hair that had tinged a slight green in the sun. She had a rounded, friendly face with pale blue eyes and full lips that bore a faint smile. Despite her youth, her intricate silk robes of blue embroidered with gold told a story of rank, power, and prestige.

"How may I help you?" she asked, her voice hoarser than anyone her age should have.

"I am a devotee of Euseeda, Sister-Wife of Tempest." He said as he bowed. "I wish permission to enter her Husband-Brother's house, holy place of Tempest and speak with his clergy. I swear upon my Goddess that I mean no ill-will."

"Enter, devotee of Euseeda, and know that you are welcomed here." The lady stepped from the archway, her arm extended him to bid him inside.

He rose and stepped forward. "Thank you."

"I'm impressed," she croaked while smiling. "It's rare I see anyone following proper etiquette around here, let alone a child of a different faith."

"I had my temple etiquette beaten into me young," Warrior replied.

The two walked to a small bench overlooking the rolling

waves. She motioned for him to sit, then sat herself. He complied.

"I am the Head Priest here, and Wavespeaker. You mentioned you wished to talk. What is it you wish to speak about?" She asked, folding her hand onto one knee and turning to face him.

He nodded. "The Shrine of Euseeda here in town is helping in the creation of some much needed magic items. Keeper and I were able to get most everything together, but we're missing a vital component. I was hoping that..." He paused as the Wavespeaker raised her hand to stop him mid-sentence.

"Did I just hear you say there's a Keeper here in town?" Her brow furrowed in a look of confusion.

"Yes," Warrior replied. "There's a Keeper here. Did you not know?"

"No," she said as she got to her feet. She moved slightly

away from the bench and gazed in the direction of the Shrine of Euseeda. "I knew there was a shrine, but thought it was pretty much abandoned. Except for its Tree, I mean."

"Have you even been there? You'd know it wasn't abandoned purely based of its immaculate grounds." He said.

"I've been there once or twice, but could not enter. I called out, but no one came forth to give me permission," She replied. "I figured it was a few of the local farmers that kept the place in working order as their offerings."

Warrior closed his eyes and rubbed his right temple. "For all his warm, caring, personality, he really is a chickenshit."

Wavespeaker's head snapped back to face him, her eyes wide. "And you said your etiquette was beaten into you?"

"The first teaching of Euseeda is honesty."

"Even if it's brutal?" She laughed.

He shook his head. "No, that lesson was beaten into me from a life on the long road."

Wavespeaker smiled and retook her seat at the end of the bench.

"Is he really?" She asked as she held her hands to the side of her head, fingers splayed.

"With four hooves, bark-skin and all," He said.

"Huh," She muttered under her breath. "I suppose I shall have to make more of a concerted effort to greet him."

Warrior sighed. "I wish you luck on that. He really is skittish. I do not know why, nor is it my place to ask."

She nodded.

"Now, back to the previous subject; magic items?" She said.

"For the last item we need to make, we need a small, waterproof container about yea-big..." He made a motion in the air with his hands, about the size of a lady's small jewelry box. "...and preferably made of gold."

The Wavespeaker's right eyebrow raised higher than the other. She crossed one arm in front of herself while she rested her chin in the palm of the other.

"What do you plan to do with this... golden box?"

Warrior sucked in his lips for a moment. "I need it to contain something. Forever."

She leaned in, studding his face and staring deep into his eyes. "Containing? Or Sealing?"

"Sealing. I was under the impression that the Temples of Tempest makes small but valuable offering in such boxes once a year. I was hoping you might have one to spare." He replied.

"You're dealing with a cursed item I take it."

"Yes."

She placed a single fingertip to the bridge of her nose and closed her eyes. "Please tell me you don't plan to dump it into Tempest's domain."

"No," Warrior said. "I had never thought of that. My intention is to take it to a place where it can be purified, if all goes well. If it goes badly, at least it can be locked away in a state it can no longer do harm. Since gold does not change states over time, it will not eventually break out of its own accord."

"You have thought this out, I see."

Warrior looked at his feet. "More so than I ever cared to."

"Well, you happen to be in luck. We do have a couple spares." She slapped her knees and stood. "But I do not offer this box freely."

"I never presumed you would," He said raising his head. "I have gold and gems to pay for its value and then some. Name your price?"

A wicked smile slowly grew across her face. "My price? Five doubloons, an amphora of the Holy Wine of Euseeda, and your Keeper actually coming out to greet me next time I come to his shrine."

A faint smile briefly appeared at the left tip of his mouth, then it was gone again.

"The five pieces, are now yours. The Holy Wine, I must check with Keeper as it is not mine to give, but I also do not see any issue with either. Frankly, he's swimming in the stuff. As for Keeper himself... Might I suggest that you, personally, go retrieve the wine? He might be a little easier to budge from his hidey-hole with a debt that needs repayment prodding him."

"You, sir, are a very clever man."

He extended his hand to her and they shook.

The midday sun was dancing between the leaves of the Great Tree and he could feel its warmth tickling his bare skin. Even with his eyes closed he could almost see the different patterns of light and dark play across the insides of his eyelids. Under him, he felt the Tree's roots gently stir, turning the ground below. On his back, he sensed Keeper's thumb tracing the last of the wards, pushing back the darkness in his gut once again.

The deep hum stopped and he opened his eyes. To his left he could see Keeper craning around from behind to look at his face.

"I guess that's it then," Warrior said, his voice soft.

"Are you sure you want to go through with this?" Keeper asked. "I've gotten better with the wards. If you'd be willing to stay, I can cast them for however long is needed."

Warrior shook his head. "Running is not the answer." He

stood, brushing traces of soil from his bare bottom. After a moment, he turned, retrieved his clothes and armor from the walkway, and began to dress himself.

"Do you really think you can win against the Liche?" Keeper removed the leather bag from around his neck and placed it to one side, never once taking his eyes off Warrior.

Warrior finished tying off his padded pants at his waist. He took a deep breath, then turned to Keeper.

"I guess we're going to find out."

Neither said anything else as he continued to dress. Padded doublet, then upper greaves, and knee guards. Leather halter, with chain skirt that extended to his calves and split in the middle and back. Another chain set that started at the shoulders then flapped down to each side of his arms, plate shoulder harness over the chain, followed by upper arm guards, lower arm guards, elbow guards. And finally the breast and back plates. His socks, and plate boots and lower greaves, however, remained untouched on the wooden walk.

"Keeper," he said after the last buckle was latched. "I wish to thank you. For your hospitality, your help and assistance in this matter at hand. I know that I would not have a chance in all the Hells if it was not for you and your Tree. May Euseeda be with you." He bowed.

"And may Euseeda bless you and your endeavor," Keeper replied.

Warrior turned and started to walk away. He stopped when he realized something had snaked around his left wrist. It was a vine from the Great Tree that held him in place. He had always known the vines could move, but he had never seen it before. And except for its roots, Thrushweaver had seemed particularly still. He looked at the Tree, then turned back to

Keeper, eyes wide and eyebrow raised.

Keeper picked himself up off the grass. However, his normally sleepy expression was gone. Instead his eyes were fully open, his pupils so dilated the green of his iris was barely visible. As he stepped closer, Warrior realized he wasn't moving the same, more proud, less skittish. No, this was no longer the Keeper he had come to know over the past week. This was Thrushweaver, using Keeper's body as a puppet.

The vine around Warrior's wrist loosened and dropped away. He stood, rigid, unmoving as Thrushweaver approached. The Tree stopped a hair's breath away from Warrior, chest barely touching his breastplate. The Tree's hands caressed his checks then took hold of each side of his head, fingers surrounding his ears. The Tree closed his eyes and pressed his forehead into Warrior's, his knot digging into the half-Elf's flesh. Black eyes snapped back open, peering deep into Warrior's very soul.

"Dalee hu maccine, ahn arie Hurraden nechit va nerehino." *Do not underestimate Hurraden, ruler of the damned.* The Tree's voice was not that of the Keeper's, higher pitched yet so much more deeper, Warrior felt it in his chest. "Mu ahn retocne astier ci horadi hu tocatchna belang sha dorlanci hassva. Eh janii ahn dalee, ishtay va caradian vicnachi ahn forfutane es. Harne va es janii ahn, orden va es tornach ahn lerni docronisa nan. Jordini ahn harne es va, sono ahn larchni es denach." *For any goodness he held in life has been stripped from him in death. Return here when you are done, for only then will you have truly won. What I and my Keeper have done to help you on your quest, has not been fully repaid. When you come back, we shall discuss final compensation.*

"Ahn nagist va es tor." Warrior replied. *That was my plan.*

The Tree kissed Warrior on his brow, hands trembling against skin, as if a parent saying goodbye to a beloved child. A moment later, the Tree was gone.

Keeper bounced nervously backwards away from Warrior. He wrung his hands for a second, then regained his composure.

For his part, Warrior remained motionless, dumb-founded by what just transpired. He knew that Trees could see and hear through their Keepers, and at least twice a year fully took them over for a small period of time for certain ceremonies, but he had never witnessed it before.

"My Tree, Thrushweaver," Keeper said, his voice cracking a little as it returned to its normal pitch. "What did he say?"

Warrior blinked before looking back at Keeper. "I thought you said your Tree had no words?"

"Between me and him, yes, that is true." Keeper clasped his hands in front of his waist. "He can only really possess language when he takes over my body. And that is not something he can do very often. To be honest, I could not understand a word he said to you."

"You were aware of all that?" Warrior sat down on the edge of the walkway by his boots.

Keeper nodded.

Warrior brushed off the dirt from his bare foot, then pulled a sock over it.

"You, my boy, need to learn Elvish."

Keeper turned to Thrushweaver, smiling softly. "After all these years together, and I'm still learning about my Tree." The distinctive clap of a sword hilt hitting the top rim of a scabbard caught Keeper's attention.

"He mostly was giving me warning about the Liche." Warrior adjusted his sword belt then reached for his shield. "And reminded me of my debt that I owe both of you for the wards. I think it was his way of telling me to be safe." Warrior slung his duffel bag back across his shoulders until it rested on top of his scutum.

"And you have everything?"

Warrior reached back and slapped his bag with his palm twice.

"Including the golden box?"

"Already filled with Holy Wine and sealed with wax for the journey." Warrior hopped down to the far side of the walkway. "Don't forget. You still have to give the Temple of Tempest their amphora of Holy Wine. Don't chicken out of that and just leave it lying around for them to take."

Warrior could hear Keeper stomp a single hoof behind him. Without looking back he walked away from the shrine and towards the stairs that lead back into town.

"Don't die." Keeper said when he reached the arbor that marked the boundary of the holy site. Warrior raised his right hand and waved behind him.

"Hey!" boomed Wavespeaker's course voice over the treetops from the bottom of the hill, "Keeper!"

Keeper winced. She was back again, like she had been every week or so since Warrior had left. While she, herself, was not a bad sort, if not a little overbearing, she brought with her the smell of briny waters that always put his nerves on a knife's edge. Still, he had learned already that ignoring her was far worse than bending to her whims, especially now she knew the Dryad was there. He rose from beside his tree and stiffly trotted over to the entrance to his sanctuary.

And there she was, this tiny human woman with all the force and power of the sea, standing just before the arbor that marked the holy ground of Euseeda. She waved vigorously when she saw him.

"I am the Head Priest and Wavespeaker of Tempest, Husband-Brother of Euseeda," she said quickly, bowing her head. "I wish permission to enter his Sister-Wife's house, holy shrine of Euseeda and speak with her clergy. I swear upon my God that I mean no ill-will."

"Enter, High Priest and Wavespeaker of Tempest, and know that you are welcomed here," He replied. His voice was flat betraying his grumpiness of having to deal with her, yet again. Yet she made no indication of noticing.

She strode beyond the arbor arch, crossed the courtyard without bothering with the provided stepping stones, then plopped herself on the wooden walkway surrounding the Great Tree. Her normally cheery face was solemn today.

"Is something wrong?" Keeper asked.

"I bring news of the world beyond our township that I think you should know," she said. "War had broken out, seven months ago. It apparently enveloped the entire region beyond the Dead Wood."

"How do you know this?" Keeper walked up to her, but made no motion to sit.

"Some sailors came in today from the sea wanting to make offering to Tempest as thanks for surviving," she replied. "Most all of them were tired and scared. They had a look in their eyes that spoke of the Hells they sailed through stronger and louder than any speech could resonate."

"We got lucky," she continued. "The mountains to the east and the Dead Wood to the north protected us from being sucked into it all. But it ended up consuming most everyone else for a good six months."

"It's over now?" Keeper asked as he leaned against one of the walkway's columns. Something in his gut twisted. He did not like where this was going.

"Apparently." Wavespeaker nodded. "Word has it a small group of mercs punched though the enemy lines and successfully took out the invader's leader in Cannondra. In the end, there were thousands dead. Lots more simply missing. Hard to really tell."

"A nasty conflict, but those happen with folk. Still, I'm glad it passed us by."

She nodded. "Doubly so since the invading army was entirely composed of undead."

Keeper felt the world suddenly drop away from under his hooves. He reeled for a moment then steadied himself. He was glad he had already leaned against the column as it kept him from simply falling to the ground. Wavespeaker was on her feet, reaching out to him, her face flooded with worry.

"Are you all right?" she asked.

"Yes..." he replied, his voice unsteady. "I... I was just not expecting that news." He knew that was not entirely true, he simply did not want to hear it.

"People are calling it the Second War of the Liche," she continued as she helped steady Keeper. She paused. Wavespeaker looked away for a moment her eyes gazing upwards and slightly to the left.

"Your friend," she said looking back at Keeper, "That half-Elf warrior, he was involved in all that, wasn't he?"

Keeper took a deep breath.

His friend. He had not realized until she had said those words. Warrior was his friend. And without looking back he had marched off months ago to face one of the greatest evils in the world, wanting to live, yet prepared to die. And Keeper had helped him. No wonder the news had hit Keeper so deeply.

Keeper nodded timidly.

"They say the mercenaries who took out the Liche King all survived and were richly rewarded. Their leader was even given the name 'Licheslayer' for his actions. You think that might have been him?"

Keeper folded his legs under himself and laid his elk belly down on the dry grass.

"It very well could be," he said, smiling and teary-eyed all at the same time. "It sounds like him, anyways."

The Warrior's Debt

The cold kept the morning mists from burning off even in the late afternoon, making visibility poor and the entire day feel gray. While it was deep winter, the coastal town was not high enough to get any snow. The Warrior was thankful for the mist. It made moving undetected much easier.

He knew he was in a sorry state. He was so cold. And his eyes no longer wanted to focus at all. A seething hunger ripped through his gut, but the concept of food made him extremely queasy. His long, waist-length, white hair he had taken so much pride in had started falling out two days ago, leaving his scalp patchy. The only things still keeping him together was the wards on his armor, and his sheer force of will.

He slinked though the winding back alleys as he slowly scaled the different levels of Echo Cove. He did not want others to see him. Best case scenario is that an observer would run away at the sight of him. Worst case, they would try and stop him. He could not afford to be halted. Not now. Not so close to his goal.

His legs lost strength and he collapsed against a stone wall, coughing. Covering his mouth with his gloved hand, he rode the fit out. After his body calmed, he pulled his hand away. It was covered in the black bile that was once his blood. Deep inside, he knew he would not last the night. He pushed away from the wall and continued to shuffle towards the upper levels of the town, his duffel bag slung across his back all the while threatening to pull him down.

The mists were thinning at the top. At the base of the stairs that lead to the shrine, they still hung around his feet. But he could see the shine itself was clear. Already, the sunlight peeking though the haze was starting to hurt his skin.

He did not want Keeper, his friend, to see him falling apart. But he had to get to the Great Tree. Halfway up the steep stairs, he stepped off the stones and into the thick wooded grove that surrounded the hill. He hid the rest of the day in the shade of the trees, waiting for nightfall. He was banking on the fact that Keeper, like many plants, functioned best when the sun was high, but tended to fall fast asleep once the sun set.

Dusk came and went. A sliver of a moon had just barely crawled over the horizon when he forced himself up once again and made his way back to the stairway. Stumbling in the dark, he finished his climb.

As quietly as he could, he entered the Great Tree's atrium. He stopped on the walkway taking a brief moment to look around. The Keeper was nowhere in sight.

"Praise Euseeda," he muttered.

He left his bag, sword belt and shield on the walkway before sitting down to remove his boots. Another coughing fit racked his body. He did everything he could to quell it as quickly and as quietly as possible. After it had passed, be began removing every piece of armor and clothes he wore. And with each piece gone, the darkness within him came lurching forward.

Bare as the day he was born, save a small wooden token around his neck, he placed the last of his clothes aside. He looked down one last time at the huge gaping hole surrounded by black, rotting flesh where his left kidney used to be. He closed his eyes and looked away. The world was becoming darker as icor clouded his vision.

He reached into his bag and retrieved a small golden box etched with wards of Euseeda and sealed with wax. He stood unsteadily and walked towards the Great Tree in the middle of the atrium. As he stepped, the grass beneath his feet frosted over, then withered from his passing. Getting on his knees, he fumbled around until he could find the offering box at the base of the tree. It took him a bit before his finger found the hole in the cover and pried it open. Inside, the roots of the Tree that made up the walls of the offering box stirred, twisting on themselves. As carefully as he could manage, he placed the gold box inside, then collapsed.

His breathing was labored and he lay on his back, facing the Tree's canopy and the cold, clear starry night above. Mustering the last of his strength, he placed his own hand inside the offering box, weakly grasping at the roots. Icor laden tears welled up, robbing him of the last of his vision.

"Oh Great Tree, Blessed of Euseeda," he began, his voice barely audible to his own ears. "I ask of you, I beseech of you, purify the wicked soul contained within. In return, I offer you, my body, my soul, my very being. Let me feed your roots so that you may, in turn, make the land fertile and the water clean. A much better fate than to be consumed by this darkness, letting this wickedness use my body to spread his malice across the land once again. Please, may this all be done, and my body gone before sunrise so your Keeper never has to see."

"All that I have is now yours," he said, pointing back to his clothes, armor, weapons and duffel bag. "Use or sell them as you see fit. My debt to Euseeda, paid in full."

Thick silence hung in the atrium. Even the night insects

were still. The Warrior's breath was now shallow, as the darkness ate at his mind.

Pain exploded throughout his body, emanating from his deep wound. For a moment, he could sense the Tree's roots burrowing inside, penetrating every fiber of his being.

Then the world stopped.

&ℭ   ℭ℞

Keeper had a very, very bad day. It was like everything he had tried to do had backfired on him. He had tripped over and broke one of his only two drinking cups. Ink from a jar he used to make notes with had tipped over, permanently staining his bed sheets. He had misjudged and cut too deep while trimming Thrushweaver's branches. And to top matters off, the extremely outgoing and overbearing Wavespeaker from the Temple of Tempest had visited today.

As a person, he really had nothing against her, per se. She was kind and courteous to a fault. But her weekly visits for some of the smallest of reasons did get on his nerves. What really got him though was her smell of salt air, briny water, and a hint of dead fish. Every time he got a whiff of her, he had to fight his own nature not to flee. That smell, it brought back too many painful memories he thought he had sealed away decades ago.

All the day's exertions, both physically and mentally, had taken their toll. Curled up on his straw bedding, his head resting on his rump, and after a bit of self-medication, he had finally dosed off.

Thrushweaver was screaming for him. The Keeper bolted onto his hooves. Sleep be damned. Now wide awake, he dashed to the door and threw it open.

Inside the atrium, by the foot of the Great Tree, lay his only friend, Warrior. And he was not well. The half-Elf's normally pale skin was nearly blue, corpse-like. His once beautiful hair spread about his head and onto the grass in mats and clumps. He looked thin, too thin, and black icor spewed from every orifice. On his left side, Thrushweaver had forced his way inside, the roots writhing and tracing their passage under his flesh. The Warrior convulsed, his amber eyes rolled back deep within his head.

"What are you doing?!" Keeper cried and he bounded off the walkway in front of his door and came to be beside the Warrior. He bent over, his hand reaching out yet stopping before he could touch. He wanted so much to just rip him from the ground and hold him, but feared doing so would kill him, if he wasn't dead already.

A wave of desperation that was not his own washed over him. He snapped his head up, knowing full well that emotion came from his Tree. Keeper forced himself to calm down, then listened with his heart.

Fear, concern, worry, followed by determination, compassion, resolve. Deep in the recesses of his mind images bubbled forth. A soul, Warrior's, on a balance scale, its pan dangling over a pit of churning blackness with rotten arms of men reaching out, grasping. The scale's arms steadied by a gnarl of roots, keeping the soul out of reach. The roots would try to move, to stretch towards the blackness, only to have the scale tip the soul towards the darkness. The roots then return and weight the scale once more to pull the soul out of danger. The watery image of Wavespeaker came to stand on the opposite pan of the scale. Then the vision was gone.

Keeper dashed from the atrium, bounded across the barely lit courtyard, only to freeze at the top of the stairs that led away from the shrine. Never once, since the day he first climbed these stairs so long ago, had he ever left this place. It was his sanctuary. Nervousness and fear gripped him as he paced there, not moving forward yet not retreating.

Another image came to his mind, forced upon him by the Tree. He was sitting in his room, the Warrior, in his full plate, with a cup of wine in hand sat across from him on a cushion.

Bravery, is not something you have or not have. It's the realization that being afraid won't save your ass.

"It's not my ass I'm scared for," he muttered under his breath. But it had given him courage. He forced himself over the edge and down the steps. Below his hooves, he could feel the roots of his tree under the roadway. Their energy pulsed though the ground in a line, as if pointing the way. Without question, he followed.

It did not take him long to find himself in front of the Temple of Tempest. The roots of his Tree stopped abruptly at the temple's coral walls. The darkness and the rolling fog made it impossible for him to see beyond the gate. He paused for a moment, his hooves clinking on the cobblestone walkway as he pranced in place, then tried to step through the archway. Something blocked him. An invisible wall stood sentinel over the archway that he could not pass through, yet the ground fog swirling about his hooves rolled onward unhindered.

He pranced again, his weight shifting nervously, his fingers coming together over and over in front and just below his human-like ribcage. As he mulled, his eyes fell upon a rope extending through the coral walls. Without a second thought, he grabbed it and gave it a good yank. Not too far off, the sharp clang of a ship's bell sounded. His ears perked up as it rang.

He pulled on the rope again, and again, and again, determined to not let his presence at the gate go unnoticed. In the distance, he could hear doors opening and disgruntled muttering. As he continued to ring, dark shapes and forms moved up through the fog. When he realized that these shapes were that of men, he let go of the rope.

The shapes paused as Keeper stepped nervously in front of the gate.

"TO ARMS!" one cried, as it disappeared back into the fog. "There's a demon at the gate, TO ARMS!"

Keeper winced.

Armored men with tridents appeared from nowhere, charging through the archway and encircling him. Keeper had to fight his own instinct to jump over them and bound away into the night. Running was the last thing he should do and he knew it. He stopped his nervous footwork, forcing himself still. Sharp points on long poles threatened him, but he stood firm.

"Begone, Demon!" said one man, with a mail shirt hastily pulled over sleeping robes. "Your ilk are not welcomed here."

Keeper opened his mouth to speak, but found the words not coming forth. The fearful pit in his gut was starting to win out over his reason again.

"Tempest Preserve! What do you all think you're doing?"

His ears perked up and a brief smile crossed his face. He knew that coarse, gravelly voice, the one that sounded like a girl that had smoked a pipe all day since the moment she was born and had been weaned on whiskey.

"Wavespeaker!" he called, rearing slightly with excitement and relief.

"That's no demon," she grumped as she pushed her way through the barricade of guards. "Am I going to have to sit you all down for a 12-hour lecture on Tempest's WIFE?"

She was a tiny thing, looking even smaller than usual when

surrounded by her temple guard and other acolytes. She was clothed in a simple blue silk shift, with a warm, thick quilted robe tossed over her shoulders and slippers on her feet. Her blonde hair was bound in braids, her head wrapped in a sleeping bonnet with a big bow tied to once side of her cheek keeping it in place. Before she could say anything to Keeper, he reached out and clasped her hands, holding them just before his breast.

"Please," he said, his fears and worries creeping into the corners of his voice. "I need your help. We don't have much time. Gather anything and anyone that would be of assistance and meet me at the shrine."

"Hold on Keeper," she replied, "What is going on?"

"My friend, Warrior. He's returned and needs help. He..." He took a deep breath, steadying his nerves again. "The Great Tree is trying to perform an exorcism and purification, but we can't do it alone."

Her face contorted slightly, her mouth pursed to once side, her brow furrowed.

"What in all the deep domains would give trouble to a Tree for purification?" She asked.

"A Liche."

Instantly she yanked her hands away from Keeper's grasp. She spun on her heels and began barking orders to those around her, demanding for holy items and personnel. A moment later, she stormed back into the Temple grounds.

"Go to your Tree," she yelled over her shoulder. "I will be there as quick as I am able!"

The Keeper nodded then bounded away.

You are MINE!

Warrior swam in blackness, fighting to keep his mind his own. The cold, horrid presence enveloped him, clawing away the last light of his existence.

"Ahn fabecci dolence ve netracsendo ordin, Vartinii." *This is an illusion within your own mind, Warrior.* He knew that voice. He had only heard it once, but he knew it as if he had heard it his entire life; Thrushweaver. The Great Tree was here, in the darkness, with him.

"*You have more power here than he wants you to realize,*" The Tree said.

Those words were an infusion from the Goddess herself. Summoning every morsel of strength, he grasped the presence and threw it away from himself. It flew some distance, then reformed.

Towering before him was the Liche, the once great King Hurraden. Bleached of all color, he was but too little skin stretched over too much bone. His crown no longer sat properly upon his brow. The once rich garb of his status now danced about him in tatters, the gems and metals of his station, tarnished and dull. His eyes were sunken, gone, replaced by eerie blue flames of pure magic.

The giant corpse of a man lunged at Warrior, clawed hands outstretched. Warrior dodged. As he did so, his own form came into sharper focus, muscle and bone and blood he knew so well. He had willed it, so it was. He felt something press against his back, hard yet warm, it pulsed with magic as if breathing.

"Please tell me you're not here as a voyeur," he asked. He shifted his stance, preparing to block. Behind him, he could feel the Great Tree chuckle.

"*I am here to help,*" The Tree replied.

Branches and roots twisted about him forming a barrier.

They glowed slightly with a warm, yellow light. The Liche circled, his flaming eyes never blinking, yet solely focused on Warrior. Warrior let go of his breath and relaxed. With the barrier in place, he felt he had a small reprieve.

"Where am I?" Warrior asked.

"*Deep within the recesses of your own mind,*" said the Tree. "*Everything you see here is your mind's own interpretation of a battle of magics and wills.*"

The Liche lashed against the wooden walls, then recoiled hissing as its own flesh burned.

"Why am I still alive?" He looked at his own hand, it too softly glowing with life in the blackness that surrounded them.

"*Do you wish to die?*" the Tree asked in return.

"I am willing to make that sacrifice if it means ridding the world of that thing." Warrior leaned back into the Tree.

"*But do you wish to die?*"

The Liche continued to circle, much like a starving wolf coming upon a lone fawn.

Of course you do, the Liche hissed. *Better that than watching forever, through my eyes, as I take your friends and family to become my new horde. Your body is MINE! The fate of your soul within, however, is still up to you.* It laughed.

A branch of the Great Tree lashed out just missing the Liche.

Give in, the Liche continued, *and be rendered to a place without pain or fear. Return to nothingness. Or defy me and be locked forever into the helpless recesses of the body once I have full control. It's only a matter of time.*

"No," Warrior stood firmly, his fists clinched. "I wish to live."

Before Warrior, a blade formed, of bark and branches, a

longsword. He grasped it by its lengthy grip and gave it a good swing. It was well balanced and weighty, just how he liked them. The magic that formed it, however did not feel like the Tree's. It was, however, familiar none the less.

"You want me to fight?" He asked.

"*I need you to fight,*" the Tree said, "*But you do not fight alone.*"

Water gurgled up around his ankles. At first the Warrior was confused, until he stood back and realized the blue-green liquid had formed a shield laying on the ground. It was a tall, rectangular shield that was curved to form a quarter barrel, a scutum. Without thinking, he stomped on the bottom edge of the shield forcing it to stand upright. His left hand grasped it by its single handle hidden behind the boss and he raised it to waist height. The water pulsed and flowed about his hand, yet never lost its shape.

"*Let Keeper's magic be your sword, and Wavespeaker's magic be your shield. Go forth and do what you do best; give me an opening to bind him.*" The barrier of wood suddenly vanished.

Instantly, Warrior charged forward, his will afire, his strength returned. The Liche met him arms wide, and tried to envelop him once again.

The Liche's scream shook the world as the Sword of the Keeper loped off an arm. It tumbled and disappeared into the blackness. Cold, blue fire erupted from the Liche and hurtled down on Warrior. He hunkered down behind the Shield of the Wavespeaker, letting the waters deflect and dissipate the magic. As soon as the fire died, he thrust himself at the Liche, scutum held in front and slamming as hard as he could into the corpse's chest.

The two spirit forms tumbled backwards. As soon as he could, Warrior got to his feet and circled behind the Liche. The Undead King spun round, refusing to give his back to his target.

Warrior smiled, and slapped the sword resoundingly against the water-shield, taunting.

The Liche screamed at him, but did not move forward. Its remaining hand clenched and the entire world suddenly shrunk inwards towards the living corpse. Warrior dug his feet into the darkness but the pull was strong.

A single sharp vine thrust through the back of the Liche's head and erupted from its right eye. The hole the vine had made became larger and larger with each passing moment as if it did not so much pierce as consume. Stopping his magic, the Undead King grasped at the vine as the green living thing continued to grow, circling around to make a go at its other eye. The second limb fell slack, Warrior's blade made quick work of separating it from the rest of the corpse.

Between Warrior and the Great Tree, they rendered the

Liche down to the shard of his essence in a matter of moments. At last, Warrior swung at the tiny blue shard with full force. It shattered, its fragments enveloped by the vines of the Great Tree and absorbed. The Voice of the Liche disappeared from his mind.

Exhausted, and in pain, he dropped the sword and shield and fell backwards back into the darkness.

℘ ☙

Keeper sighed with relief as the black icor stopped trickling from Warrior's body. He had placed Warrior's head in his lap as he weaved dusty golden signs onto his body. Wavespeaker stood at Warrior's feet, her hands clasped in front, mouth wide, her deep controlled breathing mimicking the sound of rolling, crashing water, infused with the magic of Tempest. Two of her acolytes sat on their knees to each side of her, holding offering bowls of sea water.

Warrior's body relaxed, his face stopped its contortions and fell into a sleepy trance. His skin returned to a more natural color, the purple/blue lines traced just under its surface faded. Despite this, Thrushweaver's roots were still buried deep with him on his left side.

Wavespeaker's body relaxed as well, and she let the last of her song fade. While Keeper nor she could see through the eyes of Warrior, they both very much knew what had happened, all their magic connecting them to each other.

"He still doesn't look too good," she finally said, her voice even more coarse than usual.

"He's not," Keeper shook his head. He tried as best he could to wipe the icor from the body's pale face. "My Tree is sharing his life force with him. It's the only thing keeping his heart beating."

Wavespeaker motioned to her two assistants. She

whispered something in their ears Keeper could not hear and motioned to the courtyard outside. They both nodded, rose and walked away.

"But the Liche is gone," she said coming to sit beside Keeper.

Keeper nodded.

"Is there anything else I can do to help?" she asked.

"I don't think there's anything either of us can do now," he replied, his gaze never leaving his motionless friend. "It's now up to his desire to live and the Tree's power to heal."

Wavespeaker's acolytes were back, one carrying a couple of towels, the other a deep pan filled with fresh water from the well outside. They bowed then placed the implements next to Warrior.

Wavespeaker shivered.

"It's really gotten colder," she said. "Let's at least try to clean him, then bundle him up before he freezes."

"No," Keeper corrected as he looked directly at his Tree. "Colder is better. The Great Tree thinks that it'll put less strain on his body while he tries to heal it. But a cleaning would be good."

"All right." She took a towel and dunked it lightly into the water pan. After wringing it out, she carefully started wiping away the last traces of the Liche's presence. Keeper followed suit.

"Will you need help caring for him while your Tree does its work?" she asked.

"To care for him while he is healed is my duty and mine alone," He replied. He paused and turned to the two acolytes.

"Please, would you be so kind. Behind you on the walkway, there is armor, weapons, clothes and a duffel bag. Can you take them to the storehouse?" He pointed to just beyond where his living quarters were, just past the walkway to the north. "And be careful, of the armor and swords. Those are holy relics of this shrine."

The two bowed and did as they were told.

Wavespeaker looked at him oddly. "Are you really taking away his possessions?"

"He gave them freely to the Great Tree," Keeper replied, going back to his work wiping his friend down. "His payment for assistance with the Liche. If the Tree wishes them returned, he will do so. Until then, it's best to keep them safe."

"But calling them Holy Relics?"

"What else would you call the blessed armor of the Licheslayer?" Keeper smiled softly.

He dreamt of being the land, of things living within him, through him, coming alive, growing then dying in an endless cycle. He could feel the water as it pulsed under his skin, animals and people treading on his surface. He nurtured them all, yet embraced them when their time had come. It was scary and intoxicating all at the same time. A euphoria of simply existing.

As he existed, he felt himself being pulled up and out of the earth. He twisted as he grew tall, his arms extended, reaching, grasping for sunlight and rain. The euphoria consumed him as his feet sunk back into the dirt, deep and wide. He could feel himself consume bits of the ground and water, dead decomposing things and compost, cycle through the length of his body then return, purified, cleansed. The more he 'ate' the more he hungered, burrowing, searching for more.

Around him, a male Dryad worked. He tended the soil, and trimmed his branches. The elk-man of bark and sap would talk to him, forcing his mind away from the euphoria and back to more of a conscious state. He wanted so much to reply, to sit and chat. Yet with no mouth, words eluded him. And even if he had words, it would not help as the Dryad spoke a different tongue than he had known. But his company was so welcome. It was by far, better than being alone, even in the euphoria of existing.

And thus he remained as the season slowly changed.

৪১ ৫৪

The Warrior's eyes cracked open. Everything seemed out of focus, even his mind. Deep aching pain filled every corner of his being. He tried, in vain, to move his right hand. It didn't even budge from his side. He was still alive. Yet he wondered if that was a good thing.

A fuzzy shape of cream and deep green came into his vision with what seemed like sticks growing out the sides. It took some sort of cloth, at least he thought it was cloth, and gently wiped his face. The blob placed the cloth aside then he heard the sound of something being dunked in water. He tried turning his head to see what was happening, yet his body stubbornly refused to budge.

"Can you drink?" asked the blob with Keeper's deep, calming voice.

Something wet touched his lips. It was some sort of rag that had been soaked in water, then folded to a point. Instinctively, his lips closed around the tip and he meekly sucked the water down. It was crisp and cold, nearly making him cough, but it tasted so good. Like the first rain after a long drought. The rag disappeared when it started to run dry.

"How long?" Warrior asked, his voice thin.

"You've been at this shrine for nearly four months," said Keeper. "But it was only last week that Thrushweaver was willing to let you go." The blob turned away, the sound of the rag being dunked in water returned.

The room was coming more in focus. While only being able to move his eyes, he could see enough to know where he was. He was stretched out in the Keeper's living quarters. Now that he thought about it, he could feel the Keeper's bed sheet beneath him, and the straw bedding poking up through it. Off to his right, he could just barely make out the sound of a small fire, more than likely in the cooking hearth set into the middle of the room.

He felt the cold rag return. He closed his eyes and drank. The water was welcomed relief to his parched throat.

"Do you think you can take some food?" Keeper asked.

"Broth?" he asked, letting the damp rag fall from his lips, "Or a fasting stout."

"Chicken broth," Keeper replied, removing the rag. "Any stout would be too much for you right now." He was probably right.

The Keeper propped him up, letting his back rest along the Dryad's back flanks. The Warrior's face winced uncontrollably as he was moved. Once in a semi-sitting position, the pain dulled back to a subtle undercurrent again.

He opened his eyes again as a wooden spoon was pressed to his mouth. The broth was lukewarm and slid easily down to his stomach, warming him from within. He had only finished half of the small bowl before he started to slip into sleep again.

Keeper laid the bowl aside then carefully lowered him back to the bed.

"Rest," He said. "You might be out of danger now, but you have a lot of work to do if you ever wish to hold a sword again."

Warrior smiled softly for the briefest of moments, then the expression was gone and he drifted into a deep, but troubled, sleep.

The Warrior spent far too many days in a foggy, painful dreamstate. But the pain would always wake him from his dream. And each time he opened his eyes, the Keeper was there, doting on him like some giant mother hen.

Slowly, with great force of will, his body started to respond to his commands. First his fingers, then his toes, then his arms and legs. Each time he would force himself to do more until everything stopped responding and the haziness of sleep enveloped him again.

Sometimes, he could feel one of the Tree's vines snake through the open door and come to rest on his foot as he lay. He was surprised when it first happened, but soon realized it was Thrushweaver's way of checking up on his current state. It wasn't until he was able to sit up on his own did he realize the extent of what the Great Tree had done.

New, pink flesh had replaced the necrotic hole in his left side. He felt whole. And that surprised him greatly. After all, he still vividly remembered the shape the Liche had left him in. This was more than he had ever imagined could be possible.

Once he was able to sit up, he started making real progress swiftly. Feet found the floor one day, and he forced himself to stand the next. Then walk, slowly and carefully, across the room. Then around the walkway surrounding the Great Tree of the shrine, stretching between the columns, reaching for support, until none was needed.

Warrior almost cried when Keeper added sopped bread to his thrice daily broth. A day later he was tearing into the loaf itself, consuming it all and washing it down with the broth as if a drink. The next day Keeper brought red meat, barely cooked and nearly raw. Warrior couldn't even tell if it was boar, beef, goat, lamb or venison. He didn't care. It all went down his gullet at a frightening pace.

It wasn't until a few days later it hit him. He knew the shrine had little money. And red meat was not cheap. Especially in a community where its bread and butter was fishing. He said nothing. He knew he needed the meat too much right now to help rebuild his dwindling muscles. But he worried about how much was being spent on himself, none the less.

Spring had turned into summer. Warrior took a deep breath. He stood on the walkway surrounding the Great Tree, wearing only a simple pair of trousers, his bare feet now used to the well-worn wood. From where he was, he had a clear view through the archway that defined the sacred ground, down the steps and onto the harbor some distance below. While he had been gaining strength day by day, he had not yet stepped from the shrine proper into the courtyard or beyond.

Maybe it was because of his odd dreams he had while he was healing, but he felt fearful about putting his feet on the earth. He wasn't entirely sure why. Only that he was.

Yet as he watched the port go about its daily business off in the distance, he saw a ship come in. A trade ship, the one that made regular trips here for trade and supplies. And it was a ship he knew, for it had brought him to Echo Cove before. If he ever left here, that would be the ship to take him.

He felt a longing well up within him. He had spent nearly his entire life on the long road, traveling from one job to the next. He had nothing, having given it all to the Tree in compensation for the cleansing of the Liche and his own body. But he had started with less before. He was wiser now. And had contacts in several of the major cities. If he played things well enough, he would be swinging a sword in no time. He knew he had told his closest companions he was retiring when he last saw them. But times change and he felt that if he didn't call on them for help getting back on his feet, they would be incensed.

Yet he paused at the edge of the walkway. He knew he was not yet fully healed. But he also knew he could not stay. He may be a devotee, but that was all he was. This was not his home. It was the Great Tree's home, and that of the Tree's Keeper. He, himself, had none.

He felt one of Thrushweaver's vines push against his bare back, urging him forward. He smiled, softly albeit briefly.

"Thank you," he said, without turning around and stepped from the walk to the courtyard and beyond.

It was early evening before he reached the dock, yet the sun still shone overhead. It would be a while before twilight still.

The stonework felt odd beneath his bare soles. It was unnaturally warm and buzzed slightly. He had felt it incredibly strong around the shrine, but now at the base of the dock, it was but a whimper. Yet anywhere he, or what he stood upon, was not in direct contact with the earth, like on a raised stairway or rocky ledge, the sensation practically disappeared.

As he stood, staring at the trade ship, the captain came over.

"Haven't seen you in a while," he said, lighting a pipe in his hands.

Warrior simply nodded, yet did not look towards the older human with the groomed and braided long brown beard.

"Looks like you got taken for a ride," he continued, eying Warrior up and down from under his tricorn hat.

Warrior just shrugged. Wisps of his long white hair danced in the sea breeze around his face.

"If you're will'n to work, Son, I can take you to whatever port we stop at for as far as ya want ta go." The Captain sucked a deep breath from his pipe then lazily blew out a ring of smoke.

The corner of Warrior's mouth flickered a lopsided smile. He knew the Captain was giving him a good deal, work for passage. But would he think ill of the half-Elf if he pointed out that he was probably twice the Captain's age?

Warrior continued looking out over the dock and onto the sea.

The Captain readjusted the positioning of his pipe. "You have until the late night tide to make your decision. We sail then, with or without you."

The Captain walked back to his ship leaving Warrior alone.

And there Warrior stood, thinking as the sun set. He watched quietly as the trade ship weighed anchor and drifted out to sea.

It was well and truly dark, the path of stars above reflected in the ocean and the cold of night was starting to set into his bones. Behind him, he heard the now all-too-familiar sound of sharp hooves on stone. Keeper came alongside and looked out over the water with him.

He seemed nervous, Keeper, but stood there nonetheless, his flanks twitching at the salty breeze. The two remained there for a bit, neither speaking, staring at a ship that was already over the horizon. In the end, it was Warrior who broke the silence.

"I thought you would not come down from the protection of your shrine," he said.

"Thrushweaver was concerned about you," Keeper replied, kneading his hands. "He was very insistent I find you."

Warrior nodded.

"Why did you not leave?" Keeper turned towards him, brow furrowed.

For a while, Warrior did not reply. He pursed his lips, his mind mulling over the question.

"I could not," he finally spoke, "Even though I know I should have."

"Really?"

Warrior's eyes glanced at Keeper for a moment.

"I cannot earn my keep here. Let's be honest, Echo Cove is not in need of my particular skill set." He said.

"Is money that important to you?" returned Keeper.

"Yes and no," Warrior said. "I feel my debt has not been repaid."

"I do not think Thrushweaver cares about such things." Keeper softly chuckled.

"What about you? You were the one who nursed me for the past several months. You were the one who bathed me, clothed me. It was your bed that I was laid in, your sheets and blankets, while you slept on the bare floor. It was your wood that burned in the cook fire to heat the broth, your food that you offered to me. Did you think that amount of red meat would go unnoticed?"

Keeper shifted his weight backwards, his hooves ringing softly on the stone street before the dock. He sighed.

"Money means little compared to the life of my only friend," he said.

Warrior's head snapped to face Keeper. The Dryad's admission surprised him. He felt touched.

"If you want to stay, stay," Keeper continued, "But if you

truly wish to go, I will not stop you."

He turned from Keeper, his face bent as he gazed at his bare feet.

"Honestly," he admitted, "I do not know what I want. I fully came here expecting to die. I feel like I've been reborn. But without purpose."

Keeper placed a hand on Warrior's shoulder.

"A purpose I might be able to provide," he said to his friend. "While I am very capable of taking care of Thrushweaver by myself, my ability to lead the worship of Euseeda... has much to be desired. You know the rituals. And you're far more approachable than I am for those who do come to pay respects to the Fertile Goddess of Bounty. We both would be honored if you became the Falseedo of our shrine."

Warrior blinked.

"A Falseedo? A living offering to the Great Tree? I am but a humble sellsword. I cannot claim such a high thing for myself. I am no cleric," he said, taken aback.

"You are not taking, we are offering. In a way, you already are." Keeper moved around to face Warrior head on. "In order to heal your wounds, Thrushweaver had to baptize you. While he held you, you had the dream of being with him, and the Goddess, did you not? Can you not still feel his roots beneath?"

Warrior stepped back, looking at the cobblestone around him. That odd, tickling sensation still played at the soles of his feet.

"Here." Keeper places his hand over Warrior's eyes. "Let your body relax and your mind clear. You will sense them better."

He was right. The moment Warrior let out his breath and opened his mind, he could feel them. The magic of the Great Tree was clear for him to see, branching, twisting throughout the cove and beyond. It was as if Thrushweaver stood beside them both, watching, listening, and whispering soothing words from the heart.

Eyes still closed, he raised his head towards the sky.

"Why did I not realize before?" he muttered.

Keeper patted his friend on his bare back.

"Come, let us go home. Our tree is waiting," the Dryad said, with a soft smile. Keeper turned and started to walk away, then stopped. Warrior had not followed.

Home. Such an odd word for someone who had not had one for so many decades.

Warrior looked over the town and its meandering stone streets rising up the cliff-side. Finally his gaze landed on Keeper.

"Arhun," he said, staring deep into the Keeper's green, gemlike eyes. "My real name is Arhun Licheslayer."

Keeper extended his hand.

"And I, Edowrynn."

About the Author

A long time sci-fi/fantasy geek, Smudge has had multiple comics series published at Radio Comix. She is a graduate of CalArts, and has worked in the gaming industry as an animator, written and illustrated many comic books and graphic novels, while also doing layout and web design work. She currently lives in Silicon Valley with her husband, Baron Engel, two house-mates, and copious quantities of art materials, and keeps up her hobby as an avid anime watcher.

www.ingramcontent.com/pod-product-compliance
Lightning Source LLC
Chambersburg PA
CBHW021129130626
46554CB00002B/929